T0285817

rob mclennan's On Beauty *is an a*[s] *panache, a collection of brief, ellip*[_] *virtue of their brevity, terse words* [_]

space of the page, glowing with wit, startling juxtaposition, crashing sadness, and sly comedy. For each story there is an emotional core, the thing of the story, an ordinary human thing involving birth, death, marriage, and parenthood, around which mclennan elaborates swirling arabesques of language, image, and thought. Figure and ground, object and mystery. Author as a lone skater on a pristine sheet of ice, unscrolling his mind. mclennan's sentences are elegantly dramatic and precise. He is a master of the sapient aphorism, the exquisite detail, and cascading sequences of word associations that are pure poetry. Two things to notice especially in this regard: the stories are grounded in place (Ottawa and the Valley landscape streaming by), but there are a dozen very short texts all entitled "On Beauty," together to be read as part of mclennan's strategy of contrasting and alternating figure and ground. The real, the human, and the Canadian are set inside the frame of beauty. Beauty insists. All this life is beautiful, the author says.

—Douglas Glover, author of Elle *and* Savage Love

Though I am often mistrustful of literary notions of Beauty, I am not being ironic when I say this book of stories On Beauty *is in fact Beautiful. It's a beauty attributable, in part, to the author's response to wide philosophical and literary readings over time, little threads of which wind comfortably through these almost conversational tales of everyday life in a city called Ottawa. rob mclennan, the critic, is also a thoughtful reader of poetry. It is not surprising, then, that his sentences are written with the ear of a poet, forging the painful dramas and small pleasures of the everyday lives of generations, of neighbours, in ordinary neighbourhood contexts, into an episodic suite that has the depth and complexity of a good novel. Above all, I am struck by the descriptive accuracy of the prose, the hot Ottawa streets, for example, that I also remember from childhood. The details of a certain Scottish heritage. The portrait of a city almost empty in the middle [save for the Parliament]. The relations of son to Mother, Father, children.* On Beauty *underscores once more that it takes a good reader to make good writing.*

    —*Gail Scott, author of* Furniture Music

Written in a prose style that at times is so chrome-shiny it dazzles, On Beauty *visits the vagaries of the questing mind, "the secret origins of the everyday," and the hopes, dreams, memories, and losses that burden us all. This is a superb collection.*

    —*M.A.C. Farrant, author of* Jigsaw

What is the responsibility of "building a person"? rob mclennan's On Beauty *accumulates searing questions, and delves into the deep memory of consciousness "held in amber." How might we wake from loss and conduct internal excavations? He writes: "The tricky part of our travel was in attempting to speak solo to my younger self...I woke before the narrative completed." Woven with threads of ancestral memoir, this collage of stories collects the habits of those attempting to swerve from conventions of elegy—and what comes "after." We proceed through glowing fragments: "paper dolls and Red Rose figurines...placed on every surface. Set out to safeguard." A deeply moving portrait, from embryonic scrapbooks and quotidian diaries to the many births which compose a life. A deft encounter with what happens when— "We won't allow our dead to disappear."*

    —*Laynie Browne, author of* Intaglio Daughters

On Beauty

UNIVERSITY
of **ALBERTA**
PRESS

On Beauty

STORIES

rob
mclennan

Published by

University of Alberta Press
1-16 Rutherford Library South
11204 89 Avenue NW
Edmonton, Alberta, Canada T6G 2J4
amiskwaciwâskahikan | Treaty 6 |
Métis Territory
ualbertapress.ca | uapress@ualberta.ca

Copyright © 2024 rob mclennan

Library and Archives Canada
Cataloguing in Publication

Title: On beauty : stories / rob mclennan.
Names: McLennan, Rob, author.
Identifiers:
　　Canadiana (print) 20240326644 |
　　Canadiana (ebook) 20240326652 |
　　ISBN 9781772127690 (softcover) |
　　ISBN 9781772127775 (EPUB) |
　　ISBN 9781772127782 (PDF)
Subjects: LCGFT: Short stories.
Classification: LCC PS8575.L4586 O52 2024 |
　　DDC C813/.54—dc23

First edition, first printing, 2024.
First printed and bound in Canada by
Houghton Boston Printers, Saskatoon,
Saskatchewan.
Copyediting and proofreading by
Mary Lou Roy.

A volume in the Robert Kroetsch Series.

This is a work of fiction. Names, characters,
places and incidents either are the
products of the author's imagination or
are used fictitiously, and any resemblance
to actual persons, living or dead, business
establishments, events, or locales is entirely
coincidental.

University of Alberta Press is committed to
protecting our natural environment. As part
of our efforts, this book is printed on Enviro
Paper: it contains 100% post-consumer
recycled fibres and is acid- and chlorine-free.

University of Alberta Press gratefully
acknowledges the support received for its
publishing program from the Government
of Canada, the Canada Council for the Arts,
and the Government of Alberta through the
Alberta Media Fund.

Canada   Canada Council Conseil des Arts
for the Arts du Canada

Alberta
Government

A writer is someone who knows nothing about his life or about the life of anyone else, until he has not only imagined it, but has discovered, through writing, how to imagine it.
    —*Philip Roth*

Contents

On beauty

For each time you access a memory, it changes, moving further away from the original. As Niels Bohr suggested, even to silently witness is to alter what is observed. The smell of my mother: some combination of powder and perfume. It rose from her pores. The baby is asleep.

Fourteen things you don't know about Arturus Booth

We come from long lines of people destined never to meet.
  —Miranda July, "Majesty"

1.
There is a shop in London that sells custom-built snow globes. You provide a photograph, and they return your scene in three dimensions, nestled in curved, clear glass. A light cover of permanent snow.

My friend Ian once offered that if you could imagine something, anything, there was most likely a store exclusively dedicated to it in the city of London, whether model train sets, polished stones or exotic teas from India. Ian has lived in England for more than a decade, so perhaps he would know, but until I saw for myself, I wouldn't believe him. Imagine: a diorama of you and your parents standing in your teenage living room, forever frozen in water and artificial snowflakes, a serene scene awaiting interruption. Images are all I have now. When I was seventeen, my parents died in a boating accident. They were already underwater.

2.

I am twenty-six years old. I work as an investment banker
on Bay Street. I am afraid of high places. Airplanes
frighten me. I once had a dog named Trudy. I once had a
backyard. I grew up in Oakville, just along the Mississauga
border, but now equally deny both cities. The only people
I hate more than those from Mississauga are people from
Oakville. I hate everyone from Oakville. I am allergic to
shellfish, and prefer the company of cats to the company
of dogs. I nearly married the first woman I slept with.
There had been intervention. In hindsight, I'm glad for it.
It took many years for me to come to this conclusion.
Small children confound me. I have many friends,
although I rarely see any of them.

3.

My parents went into the water. My elder and sole sibling,
Alice, was called to identify. I remained in her car, held in
amber. Perhaps, a vise. Our parents, not-alive and not-
dead, Schrödinger's quantum design. Alice stepped into
the hospital, instantly killing them. She stepped into the
room. After forty minutes, she returned, red-faced. Blush.
Alice started the car. She said only that they looked
distorted, not like them at all, but still them. She said
nothing else for a long time. We went out for seafood,
missing the irony.

What I recall. Memories merge, lose distinction. There
was snow on the windshield. We arranged for their bodies

to be flown back north, home. It sounds more benign than it actually was. Another four months before ground thaw, to break through the surface to bury them. Drifting snow sparkled on the windshield. Accumulating, as we sat in the funeral home parking lot. We, too, would be buried, had we remained. Had the base of the world only shook, would the flakes have risen from the surface, to drift down again?

At that moment, I felt the earth move. Now-falling snow, dislodged because of it.

4.
Thump. The blood vessels under my right eardrum, thump, intermittent. A distracting pulse. Perhaps you require a hot shower, my fiancée suggested. What? I answered.

Something happened last year and my left hand began to blister. Some part of my wrist in a tourniquet, pinched, as the ridges and definition swelled smooth. I was afraid of the change, and yet fascinated. After a few days, it began to reshape, down to what I knew as familiar, but with a healthy new bruise on the back of my hand.

5.
When my mother's father was a small boy in England, his own father died in a mining accident. A hill gave way and folded, deep as a mouth. Too small to understand, the boy

not yet my grandfather pointed fingers at embankments, cooing his father asleep in the rise. Every earthwork, the length and the breadth of the countryside, as big as the hole that his father left. Even as he grew into maturity, there was a part of him that always imagined his father in restful sleep, underneath a lone hill. Like Arthur, the king from his picture books. I was named for this childhood misunderstanding, this unnatural and misplaced hope. When I was born, my mother told me, he insisted I had my great-grandfather's eyes, risen and finally awake.

6.

I do not like anyone touching my feet. This is visceral, volcanic. I have not felt the need to dig too deep to inquire why.

7.

Before our parents died, I saw a young woman on the subway with a vintage suitcase. The sides were alive with scratches, worn and beige. It rested between her feet on the dark-coloured floor, and her left hand kept rising to meet with strands of her hair, greeting them back into place. She was remarkably beautiful, I remember. Full red lips, sparkling eyes. Tight black jeans, and a loose-fitting T-shirt that suggested deep curves. I wondered what such a woman might carry in such a briefcase. She guarded it carefully, casually. Almost distractedly.

Close to one of the stops, some younger boys began roughhousing, pushing into each other, a joke that quickly went

too far. I was jostled, as was she. The car doors swished
open. I regained balance, grabbed the suitcase, and bolted,
until I ran breathless. I ran for six blocks, finally certain I
hadn't been followed, and slipped into an alley to study
the contents.

The suitcase was empty.

8.

One day this will all be yours, my grandfather offered.
He'd been decreasing steadily since entering the nursing
home, five years alone in this room. Six months after the
morning of his shaky pronouncement, he passed away in
his sleep, a culminating series of little strokes into a single,
final rupture. His store had long been sold, and the building
transformed to condos. What belongings he'd accumulated
were in storage, a steamer trunk packed with photographs,
letters, dusty books, some of my mother's toys.

I haven't yet deciphered what he might have been refer-
ring to.

I had been afraid to ask, directly.

9.

Against my will, a busy Saturday late-night at a nightclub
dubbed The Fire Station, decorated with bright paraphernalia of red helmets and hoses and posed photographs,
I pulled the fire alarm, convinced it was a prop: it wasn't.

10.

What strange humour our parents had. My mother, a professor at the university, specialized in Victorian children's literature. What most recall first: her fixation with Charles Dodgson, who wrote under the name Lewis Carroll, and who swelled with his own, dear Alice. As our parents named us, Alice and Art, each name punctuating the sound of short *A*.

At the hospital morgue, my sister was forced to identify our parents, and she tumbled deep down the rabbit hole. She would spend years there. It was the change that made all that followed different, she claimed.

The Red Queen. Off with her heart.

11.

As a younger man, my grandfather in dry goods, a general store in what once was a hamlet, absorbed during his tenure into the larger morass of suburbs and extended city. A store by himself, and the small apartment above where he raised my mother, beyond the death of his wife. His days spent in retail, my mother a girl underfoot, wrapped up in her stories of magical creatures living and playing in corners and cubbies of every small outlet. The mornings he climbed down the stairs to put the kettle on and unlock the front door, discovering her array of paper dolls and Red Rose figurines she'd placed on every surface. Set out to safeguard, whatever might have come.

12.

Now, on the Canadian side of Horseshoe Falls, Niagara,
I hand strangers my digital camera, politely request
they snap pictures of me and Lucinda, each one arm
embracing the other. We are soon to be married, a
weekend away after a conference at Brock University in
nearby St. Catharines, leaning now against metal railing
and borderless mist. Lucinda, who dreams in books, and
sings softly under her breath, when she thinks no one can
hear.

We are taking pictures, drafting our permanence.

I am already dreaming this image in miniature: three
dimensions, surrounded by snowy water.

Interruptions

Her memory shot through every age, simultaneously, back to front and front to back, the eternal through the heart of the ephemeral.
　—Andrew Steinmetz, Eva's Threepenny Theatre

1.

Alberta had a moment when she remembered everything: she remembered the smoke in her hair, she remembered the smell of his skin. It was as though she'd been startled from a deep sleep of decades, suddenly realizing where she actually was.

The slight fragrance of moisture through the kitchen window, ajar. The fresh April air pushing out the last remnants of winter.

　Petrichor: after a droplet of rain strikes dry earth, the scent that releases. In part, from the Greek *ichor*, a fluid that flows in the veins of the gods. Rain. The smell, reducing her to near zero. The quality of dust in the city nowhere near that of home. Alberta is immediately home.

Scent is the strongest trigger to memory. Alberta is nearly knocked over.

2.

Alberta wrote novels as naturally as others drew maps, and with as much precision; each sentence as clear as lines sketched by James Cook, Samuel de Champlain or Simon Fraser.

Alberta compared herself to an explorer, writing to clarify the unknown.

She had enjoyed a fair amount of success, with multiple jaunts on the festival circuit for each title, including book clubs and foreign tours, and even a shortlist or two.

She still hadn't forgiven David Thompson for mapping the forty-ninth parallel, the four days he lost track of which side of the border he stood on. The mistake made her distrust him in everything.

She pored through his journals, felt for his wife, and scoffed at his editorializing.

3.

The fourth time around, the cancer had spread to his bones. Graham wore a blue handkerchief to cover his modesty, and Alberta is sleeping with one of the neighbours.

She suspects there are no worse betrayals.

Suspects, but not enough to stop.

In her life so far, Alberta can't decide if everything happened too fast, or if the whole story is set in slow motion.

Thick-headed, wilful. She shakes cobwebs loose. She shakes loose excuses that rain torrents around her, filling the kitchen, the office, the dining room.

Excuses, enough she could drown in.

When Graham's diagnosis looked terminal, he had offered permission and she had denied him, denied it, said no, no, never. Something quiet, he suggested, in that way he had. Saying all he needed by speaking less.

A woman has needs. A kindness. She said no. Not long after, she did. He gave her permission and, in return, she lied.

Lied, lied down. She did lay.

4.

Emily descends school bus steps, walks the half block home with her small group of friends. Sometimes, Alberta suspects, this group of girls share little but age and geographic circumstance. Is that enough? Perhaps it doesn't matter. These girls with her Emily, each as foreign and confusing to her as her own daughter. All squealing, high-pitched. As though they had each emerged from separate species, on either side of human. There is far too much pink for her liking, far too much talk of princess dresses and reality television, gossip surrounding useless pop stars and their crises.

Alberta flies off the handle, regularly. So much so, to Emily, it seems that her mother might never land. Perpetually in mid-air. Hovering.

When Alberta explodes, Graham responds by speaking Alberta's name. The tone of his voice a slow and gentle anchor.

Emily enters the house with a step heavier than her small form might suggest, the pounding weight of each foot.

In her bedroom cocoon, Emily absentmindedly tears fingernails across her left forearm, constructing a scar out of something smaller, neither of which even existed the day before.

Emily is carving out holes in the air.

5.

When she first discovered him, Graham had the most luxuriant brown hair. To Alberta, he was himself like the mythical Greeks: immortal, chiselled and passionate. She fell for his beauty, and remained for his kindness. He had such a rich, inner warmth that his attractiveness nearly fell away. Nearly, but not.

And for a long time, she knew she was blessed.

She knows: she drifted because she was a coward. Afraid to watch her husband die, instead falling further, into another man's arms.

Another man, who might barely be that. The occasional love poem appears in her inbox, heartbreakingly earnest, and painfully mediocre. All that keeps her: the fact that she stopped reading them.

6.

Their Emily, firstborn. Named for the books her mother had loved. For that exotic girl on the opposite coast. Tales from an island. Named, and hating it. Emily wished to be self-created, rise herself up from the earth, fully formed.

She wished for neither father nor mother.

She arranges her dolls and stuffed animals in her bedroom into a precise pecking order. Brown bear behind stuffed white rabbit beside velveteen replica. Every thing in its place.

Still. There was something restless in her that she couldn't explain. The irony of what Emily didn't know: had her mother recognized the signs, Alberta could not only have explained, but have named it.

The same name she'd given to hers.

7.

Alberta stepped into the water. The pool held no surprises, a routine of quick dip and rinse after thrice-weekly workout. She stepped and slipped in, allowing cool chlorinated water to engulf her. Her wet, crinkled feet webbed at the poolside. Alberta immersed, she pushed off from one side, propelling her body like an arrow.

Alberta: a knife through clear water.

Below the surface, there was no smell of her lover's dark skin or her in his hair, or her husband's disease. Already the smell of death rose from the bowels of the house itself, and left traces on everything, including her clothes and her fingertips, her papers and books, every morsel of food.

During his chemotherapy sessions, she had taken to eating in the deli down at the corner, far away from the infection of so much decay.

Once there, she would eat untainted food, and then pull out her notebook, spend an hour or three spinning her wheels. She couldn't gain traction.

No matter what words she wrote, she couldn't touch ground.

Bicycle

But did she return?
  —*Gail Scott,* The Obituary

1.

He paints a bicycle on her shoulder blade. Etches. The needle cadence, carves. Her red utility design, a bicycle like hers. He stretches canvas skin.

She is topless, lying on her stomach, and paying for the privilege of each pained expression.

An hour passes. Three.

Ottawa is too hot for anything. A heat advisory. Rideau wishes, wash. She pays her money and walks; itself, a rarity.

It is muggy, warm, and underneath her bandage sweat, an unbearable itch.

2.

Six-hour block, her evening job, coffee shop. Shifts, she stands. Her shoulder throbs. Order, change and cup. Order, change and cup. Shifts include junkies in the washrooms. Too often, staff scraping blood from beige walls.

Ugly service industry. Shouldn't be so fucking hard. Muzak, soft. When no one notices, she turns the satellite to something more palatable. Something with an edge.

She groans out lattes, chillers, americanos. The window washers, you could set your watch.

The hours melt, a seeming mass.

3.

She has been attempting to catch the attention of the girl in the apartment below hers. Blonde, curved, university age. She hovers at the window, alert to how the house breathes, exhalations as the front door opens, shudders. She hears movement. Footfalls, creaks, the downstairs kitchen cupboards. House-breaths rattle her apartment door the slightest, ripple. If the house was a body, the hallway and the staircase might be lungs.

She hopes to catch, an eye. A simple glimpse. A purse of lips.

A week prior, she ran quick fingers through their shared apartment dryer, skin against her neighbour's clothes. She daydreamed. A little creepy, sure. But the fabrics were so warm, and soft.

4.

She knows there are two kinds of people: cat people and dog people. Everything comes down to this.

There are no "bird people," simply self-hating cat people, or dog people who don't think they deserve to be loved.

Specimen, the cat, tears into her skin. Spec. The clipper pares his front claws, never makes it to his hind legs.

He squirms, slices, escapes. She yelps in pain, surprise, release. His cries a mix of anger and such deep betrayal. He catches carpet, slips beneath a chair.

She heads to the bathroom, washes cuts and scrapes, her blood. Returns to offer him a treat from the kitchen as apology.

Decides she will reattempt, tomorrow. He does not understand.

5.

Tucked away, apartment turret. Her cuckoo clock, exhumed from antique salvage. Discarded doorknob. She knows the importance of tokens. A guitar pick rescued from the sticky black of club floor, used onstage by Andy Stochansky. A blue scarf gifted from her favourite aunt, plucked from her favourite Parisian shop, when she was ten. A jar of smooth stones collected from the beach in Cobourg, when she was fifteen. The tales her father told along the boardwalk, of the summer when he was fifteen, strolling the same beach.

6.

Canada Day, 11 a.m. The downtown core empty of human activity but for revellers, in big red. Abandoned office towers, dark shops. Flags descend, draped as cowls, capes. Rare cars doppler. Centretown, toward the Hill, toward the Market. The occasional OC Transpo bus. She rolls her lengthy way down. Bicycle slow.

Snowbirds, overhead. A quintet swish, and smoke trails.

Parliament Hill, the hole that must be filled. Groups gravitate toward the centre, a Capital nexus that strengthens throughout the day. Gravity, it pulls and pulls.

She, too, almost aimless. Catcalls from the occasional balcony along Somerset, indirect cheers from a patio group at the Royal Oak at Gloucester. Empty spaces fill.

What is a country? Her references are not the same.

Pamela Anderson's birthday. Canada's Centennial baby, from Ladysmith, British Columbia.

You can't blow up the earth. A line she recalls from the animated series, *The Tick*. That's where I keep my stuff.

A woman, from the waist up, sporting only stickers.

7.

She pulls along, aside. Ties her bike on York Street, locks. Horse, up to the hitching post.

Torn, the way she paces. Anxious, parse. Chains her heart up to a metal post. Leaves it, here, where she might just be. No matter.

Bicycle, candy-apple red, with Granny-Smith green trim. A birthday present from her mother, three years. Three years since cancer withered her body, and stole her away.

She steps, into the steady dark. The series of daytime drinkers in the Dominion Tavern, unaccustomed to this rare weekday deluge of patrons. They know something is wrong, but they couldn't say what. The old and young alike.

Recollecting, this once "Dominion Day," celebrating, what. Dominion. Over what, she does not understand.

Bartender pulls a pint and passes, over. She sits to read her book. She, quiet.

Her friends will be there, soon. Sooner or later.

8.

The Dominion Tavern, big screen plays a documentary on golf and mentorship. Overhead blasts audio, the Pixies, *Surfer Rosa*. She is entirely too comfortable. She reads her book, and waits.

Punk kid strolls over from the pool table. Aims to interrupt her reading. Bartender silent, floats by with the back of the hand, deflects. They know her here.

Her friends arrive. She slips her book away. Mary Ruefle, *Madness, Rack, and Honey*. They pool, collect in the corner of back patio.

Pulls a pint and passes, pulls another. She swims in Kichesippi, Beau's, a local wash. She genuflects for local flavour.

Older than she looks. The late-night rain begins to fall. Warm, on their faces.

9.

Midnight, fireworks. Mouth presses mouth, outside. She,
and she. They'd ignored the official display, now catch the
whistle-squeal of ruin, releasing packets of individuals
in brush, a counsel of trees, beside apartment trestles
from the Byward Market east into Sandy Hill, low-income
dwellings. The whistle-squeal and pop, most often followed by the strawberry swirl of sirens. Police cars, run.

She pictures happiness. The colour green.

10.

A bicycle, like hers. An empty post, broken chain. Her
mother is dead.

On beauty

The English novel began as a correspondence. Bram Stoker's *Dracula*, composed as a sequence of letters between characters, combined with journal and diary entries. The novel as personalized pastiche. A thousand years earlier, Murasaki Shikibu's *The Tale of Genji*. Who is the intended reader for the contemporary novel? Some books are composed to be intimate. Is that better, or worse? Perhaps an improvement to be spoken to directly, as opposed to listening in to a conversation between others.

The snow fell in large, furious flakes. Drifting, lazy. Accumulative. She named it a "snow-globe Saturday." I had the kettle on. The air water-thick. She felt every hour of those thirty-six weeks. She felt every jostle and kick. I was beginning to see them more clearly, fleshy outline of baby-foot in my dear wife's belly. There was something inside. We were building a person, someone who would emerge and eventually go to school, find employment, drive a car, find a partner. Once they're old enough, the possibility of grandchildren. But let's not get ahead of ourselves. We were building a person. There can't be any deeper responsibility. There can't be anything so rewarding or so terrifying. Thirty-six weeks. And her nausea remained.

In my journal, I wrote: The knowledge of freedom is the invention of shape, the invention of escape.

The Matrix Resolutions

I can't translate myself into language any more.
—Alice Notley, Culture of One

1.
Plot leads the mind in a particular direction, and often
turns. The twist.

Weekly until my daughter turned seventeen and started
working, we saw new feature-length films in theatres,
followed by a late lunch. Each opening Saturday, padded
seats nearly empty at the noontime showing, with dozens
lined up for 4 p.m., or 6. Why wait?

We watched movies. We watched them unfold.
Overloaded with popcorn, but exclusively without butter.
She wouldn't dip her hands in oil.

After a decade of watching films, I asked what she noticed
first: story, setting, dialogue. She replied: Everything.

2.
I can't explain the depth of my disappointment with the
third film of the Matrix trilogy, *The Matrix Revolutions*.
It veered enough from the path set by the first two that it
contradicted.

For centuries, it was said, the Chinese didn't record their
history, believing it to be cyclical, where every point
would return. Is this what the Architect meant, when he
gave Neo that choice? Implying that Neo wasn't a blip
in the system but built-in. That he wasn't the first to be
allowed the non-choice, to walk through the door he was
offered and re-start the human colony with a small group
of his choosing. Begin again. It was the choice he was built
for, a system reboot. When he wouldn't follow direction,
would the system self-destruct?

Which leads to the question: Who made the previous
choice? Zion's Councillor Hamann, who offered advice,
and visible restraint. What he may have been forbidden
to tell.

What are facts but stories that have been told enough
times to solidify? To turn to stone.

3.
A memory: my daughter takes photographs. Twelve years
old, she caresses the digital camera, a weight in her palm.
Holds it up like an orange, prized.

She stands in the yard. A few considered minutes to set
up each shot in her head, turn and step aside. Once each
image is captured, she studies the screen. Memorizes. I
watch her look at the garden, look through every angle. A
wonder to behold.

In the space of an hour, she takes eight photographs in and around the tiger lilies, tomato plants.

4.

An argument suggests the most pervasive way to affect culture in the 1890s was through the poem. Within a couple of decades, it had shifted to the novel. By the 1960s and 70s, it had become film, before shifting to television. Now, one might say, it would be through video games, although streaming might be in the running.

Is freedom, really, the possibility of isolation?

5.

The Matrix trilogy, set in an undesignated future, when all but a few are enslaved by intelligent machines. They, in turn, fed and fuelled by human energy, human resistance. They thrived on conflict. Structures implanted so deep, beyond conscious choice into nature, for machine, human and program populations. That there would be but One, or could be.

By the end of the second film, Neo broke not the chain but direction. There would be Another. To be replaced by his unborn child with Trinity, and thus, would be, briefly, three. Her dual nature, divided in two.

One and Another, neither of whom could exist side by side. To end the unbreakable chain.

Like Moses, he would have to die so the rest could reach the Promised Land.

6.

Overheard in the pub: I loaned him a dozen movies, and he still hasn't watched them. Why read the book when you could just watch the movie?

In the men's washroom, a patron has abandoned the newspaper, again.

7.

Hugo Weaving's Agent Smith. An insistence of ego.

A friend's anger at the communal dance, more sexually charged as the scene unfolds. The pacing of a family movie, suddenly akin to an orgy.

Rain: the water branches, coils. Heavy rain. This is where stories begin.

The Garden

My sentences do get under their skin.
   —*Gertrude Stein,* The Autobiography of Alice B. Toklas

1.

He measured his days in rows of pulled, purchased earth.

David studied his garden. The worst summer in decades, the driest the valley had seen. He fought a heroic battle against weather, the passage of time. What the squirrels hadn't dug up, destroyed or outright stolen, had withered.

The gutters like margins. A layer of dust.

The plants on the back deck opposite his grew higher, greener, lush. He wondered: Was it the lack of deck covering, allowing more sun? Did his neighbour water her plants more often? Did she know how to coax, to grow deeper through pruning or chemical encouragements? Did she, unlike him, simply know what she was doing?

He sat in his one comfortable deck chair, reading a book on the Battle of New Orleans. On page fifty, the British raged; on page seventy-three, Andrew Jackson raged. Everyone raged.

The rain came, and the water boiled.

David, rainless. He sat in his deck chair, and imagined his neighbour gardening, perhaps in the nude. He wondered what she might look like naked. Perhaps much like every other woman he'd known.

2.

There was a time, David knew, the world hung upside-down. After the towers, imagining men that no longer fell, but held, in mid-air. There should be no more falling. Nor could there be. All that had fallen had already landed.

Madness overwhelms, yet reason is lighter. Returns to the surface. Does this make him an optimist, or something else?

The apartment was stuffy, impossible to breathe. At least outside, the pretense of breeze. So hot so hot so very hot. The barometer rattled.

Moisture left his body, and evaporated.

David studied the sky. It was entirely cloudless, a deep baby blue.

3.

From within this July midday heat, David timed his trek to front door to the mailman's arrival, and discovered a small sleeping bat in the hallway, beneath the landlord's mailbox. The spring bats only learning to fly, disoriented, seeking out the cool places. David retrieved his gardening gloves, gently lifted the furry bundle, set it loose in the yard. It released a couple of chirps and flapped off, swallowed by neighbouring maples.

The following morning, the newspaper reported on the influx of bats, distracted by the extreme heat, ending up in unusual places. They might enter your house. A photograph graced the front page of the *Ottawa Sun* of the "flying fox," a tropical fruit-eating variety. A far more frightening image than the meek Canadian mouse with wings.

Why would the paper depict this, a creature impossible here? Did the lie of the fruit bat seem more sensational?

Danger, Will Robinson. Danger.

4.

From his shaded perch, he could make out tattoos of small birds down the length of her left arm as she gathered ripe baby tomatoes. Her long straight hair strayed in the breeze.

She was distant, close. He suspected this might have been the allure.

He picked a snow pea and bit, let flesh crunch between molars. He preferred the raw scent and taste.

A quote from Gertrude Stein, that she wrote for herself and for strangers. David wondered if he might be one of those strangers.

5.

Apparently some hereto unseen writings by Marilyn
Monroe had recently surfaced, including the revelations
of her literary aspirations. What might they have found?
Unexpected, but hardly a shock. The newspaper colum-
nist's barely held gasp.

How could anyone be surprised? After all, she married
a playwright.

But the argument fails, holds no water. Do we know if she
ever wanted to play professional baseball as well?

Memory cares not what it gives back, or covets. In the
end, Marilyn left.

He refolds his finished newspaper. Inside, his third-
storey steam-bath, twenty degrees hotter than outside.
Half his closet was bare. Between half and two-thirds.

Beware celebrity, he warned himself. The nights now see
so few stars for the proliferation of dim-witted light. The
pollution of bulbs.

6.

David watered his plants, filled lime-green watering can
deep from the bathtub faucet. At least the water advisory
hadn't yet reached them.

If Billy has three tomatoes, and Sally gives him two more,
how many tomatoes will Billy have?

This is why school texts use apples, instead. Billy couldn't care less. The internet meme that asks, if Billy has fifteen chocolate bars and eats eight, what will Billy have? Diabetes, I'd wager.

In his deck garden, David's plastic planters are clay-coloured, allowing the appearance of classical weight. Snow peas, lavender, beets, parsley, tomatoes. The black squirrels had dug up his bulbs, leaving scraped-empty pots. They even pulled up the poisonous ones, tearing debris to shreds.

And he wonders: Given they chewed through a poisonous bulb, is it wrong to have expected them dead? Must the punishment always fit the crime?

On beauty

In a dream at the edge of consciousness, I was time-travelling with my wife, attempting to show her what I was like when I was younger. I wished to inform my younger self: It will get better. Is that all I wanted? It will get better. It did. The tricky part of our travel was in attempting to speak solo to my younger self, without attracting the attention of parents, classmates or teachers. From a distance, I attempted to catch the eye of my pre-teen self on the public school playground, from the edges of brush. Did I find myself? What did I say? I woke before the narrative completed. I have not thought of that playground for a very long time. The method in which we travelled was never revealed. I would like to know how it might have played out.

Swimming lessons

Tomorrow didn't ask me what was, what will be my life.
—*Nicole Brossard,* Intimate Journal

1.

She was loath to admit, but she dreaded the lake.

Instead, what compelled her: their shared preference for gin and tonics. Tanqueray, the scent on her father on Sundays. Bombay Sapphire, the ironic sweet taste of colonialism. Beefeater, far too dry for her palate.

Emily sips, and thinks of England. She had begun to hate England.

British army generals of the Boer War acting as though on holiday: each their iceless mix, sitting furthest from front lines. The undrinkable water.

Why was the water undrinkable? She speculates: cholera. The details of her grade-ten history studies, long slipped from their moorings.

But for now. Someone pours her another. Another.

Everything depends upon a long, late-summer weekend with friends, five women in a cottage in the Gatineau Hills, the margins of Meech Lake. Just out of sight of the nudists.

The ends of her marriage. Her shoulders tense as she grasps a fresh tumbler.

2.

Numbers dislodge from the face of her pocketwatch. Five
loose, to where gravity set. The watch functioned only as
long as numbers were clear of the hands. Time progressed
at the same rate, but too often stalled, caught.

Time ground to a halt, and nothing would happen.

She could no longer depend on it. She sipped at her drink.

She sat by the lake, adjective versus noun.

3.

The margins of lake, and this cottage. What few knew,
how some beaches have to be constantly replenished,
otherwise they erode completely. Sand down to clay down
to stone. Back up a truck to the shoreline, and smooth.

Sleepy cars in the driveway, nestled in gravel.

A rare piping plover skips across sand. So far from the coast.

The whole of the Summer Olympics, a bear trap of memory. Someone always needed to be fourth. Somehow
worse to be fourth than dead last.

Tore a muscle, mid-stride, and that was the end of her.
Without even an endorsement.

Those awful thoughts, wishing for someone else to dis-
qualify. At least a disqualification ahead of her would have
meant bronze.

Two summer games since come and gone, and now she's
no more than a footnote.

Hope is the worst thing they can give you.

4.
Deep in distracted thought, she sticks out the tip of her
tongue. As did her mother, someone points out.

There was the lake, and then not-lake. Beneath the trees
you could not tell the difference. A patchwork of ducks
float by in a crescent, akin to slow-motion buckshot. A
wave of mosquitoes, or sparrows.

Internet memes. The cassette mixed tape and the Bic pen,
courting nostalgia: who remembers?

Water, lake. They glide.

5.
She recalls the obvious charms of Eddie "The Eagle"
Edwards, the British ski jumper who competed in the
Olympics, and always placed last. He enticed the public
and world media, and was the first sports star she'd
noticed. Six years old, in front of the heft of her mother's
archaic console television. As though failure his greatest
achievement.

A book on Sarah's summer bookshelf: *I could not love a human being.* She laughed out loud. The title could not have been more appropriate.

She tries to blur, fall away from description. Attempts compression. Someone mentions a playlist, and music bubbles up from hidden speakers. David Bowie, "Heroes." Susan mentions how they are all old enough to remember being handed cassettes of curated pop songs. Once a month, Susan informs them, she still compiles mixed CDs for her friends, and sends them through the post. She does this entirely because it feels antiquated, she claims.

She was the cartographer, attempting to articulate the map of her distress. No, she thought. Too overwrought. She was muddled and messed up, as simple as that.

To throw a stone, a woman must be lithe. As if, at will, she is able to actually curl her feet, upturn toes like a fiddlehead. Think of the death of that poor Wicked Witch crushed by Dorothy's house. Made up of muscle. Muscle, sinew, and bone. Made of a steel eye and steady hand: pitch-perfect aim.

There was a religion she'd heard of, akin to a cult, that followed the belief that humans don't require any more nutrients than what can be taken in from the air and the sun. Breathers, so called. She would take breath and live. Reclining in the direct line of summer flare, she could almost believe them.

6.

What she had etched on the inside of his gold band: Put this back on.

At the ceremony, as he read it aloud for the first time, everyone had a good laugh. And then he put it on.

7.

Her friends on the deck with the patio door ajar, two or three who keep track via Twitter of women's weightlifting trials. The sounds drifted like sugar in water, swirling twice before being absorbed into crisp, late-summer air. Gail calls from the living room, wonders if their brown leather belts functioned like those coloured scarves from French voyageurs down the Grand, to hold in their hernias.

The flex and the strain and the push, until something is finally forced to give.

She knows they take turns in the kitchen, on their iPhones checking stats and scores. Each new drink, an opportunity. Let me get that for you, they offer, lifting her glass.

Women's swimming. Air bubbles caught in the contours of swimsuits, cleaving their way through clear blue.

They swoon over Michael Phelps. Smoke on the water.

8.

The parable ran that the lake crater was created by a retreating glacier, shaving back the skin of the earth.

Scraping Canadian Shield, carving ruin, an abrasion overflowing with water.

Once the glaciers of the northern half of North America warmed, the surplus flooded most of Europe, nearly ending the earth's brief experiment in humanity.

Now mountain ranges rest where ice once lay twenty miles deep. A triangle of Scottish hills with equal shelf, scraped. A line drawn, as it were.

She pushed and pushed and pushed until she broke. Her body raged, bubbled back to the surface.

She inched into the water. A day's worth of drink in her skull, she submerged, and forced air from her lungs. A cool that froze solid, down to the bone. The blood in her veins cooled to slush. A cold that, once familiar, warmed.

Water, water everywhere. She kicks off her swimsuit. Frees wedding ring from ring finger.

What she knows of whale music, sound waves travelling miles beneath the water's surface, undiminished. Audible, still, even if none around to listen.

Underwater, which she prefers to compare to the vacuum of space. Where no one can hear you.

Character sketch

The days dragged on, and I couldn't stop thinking about her.
    —*Paul Auster,* Man in the Dark

1.

What frightens us most isn't death, but its result: absence. Memory shapes and makes us, constantly shifting and changing. We are never the same for very long. If humans are the only animal with a connection to even the concept of history, how couldn't absence overwhelm? We dream up vampires, ghosts, the zombie apocalypse.

The dark side of longing. We won't allow our dead to disappear.

From Romanian folk tales, we learn that suspected vampires were buried in rice-packed coffins. If the dead were to rise, they would first be compelled to pause, to count every grain. The cemetery caretaker would have time to act, decapitate the corpse with a shovel. Separately, bury the head.

These stories fail to explain why vampires have such innate compulsion, or how a craving for blood relates to numbers. A possible blood count. On *Sesame Street,* the purple-skinned Transylvanian, Count von Count, rolled numbers off his felt tongue with ease. More often, without invitation, or ability to stop. Obsessed.

For the record: I hate the zombie apocalypse. If there is an apocalypse, it will come from the living.

2.
At the National Gallery, I stare into the skin of a painting. I stare into layers of oil.

The landscape inside a cat's head.

Delilah's scissors and Samson's hair. Like St. Patrick's snakes, his hair may have been metaphor.

I ease toward the basement galleries, the permanent home of the Inuit exhibits. A hand-held knife swims through the flesh of a harp seal, providing not just for the hunter, but for the village. Black face and silver-grey, the seal bleeds, pencil-drawn. Fixed.

Neil Armstrong, who takes that first step on the surface of Earth's moon, now and forever. Our sun, Sol, most likely knows it's a star. It's we who have skewed perspectives.

Small, so small, so very small.

3.

I have yet for my father to offer his take on the birds and the bees. Thirty years late. Now that my son is eleven, I want to have an idea of what I should tell him.

A knowledge discovered through trial. I don't want to frighten the boy.

On my usual Friday, I collect him from day camp, held at a youth centre deep in the village. This was his mother's idea. When I arrive, twenty-five children are jumping in place, singing songs about Jesus. The young woman in charge wears a hula skirt over her own, and one of the teenage staff is dressed like a pirate.

What have hula skirts and pirates to do with Jesus?

I'm uncomfortable with such blatant indoctrination. Shouldn't one be able to impart a moral centre to children by example, and not through repeated folk tales of a Jewish man some two thousand years ago who may or may not have existed?

I wouldn't exactly offer you up as example, his mother chides.

4.

Moira, my second wife, hand-picks a paperback copy of *How to Take Charge of Your Fertility*. I wonder: Who is in charge of it now?

She responds: This is entirely the point. Her eyes sing: Stop talking.

This, a position I did not expect to be in, twice. The distance is startling. The distance one travels and has travelled.

I want to have a baby, she punctuates. What I already knew.

5.

A single newspaper column announces that puppeteer Jerry Nelson, the voice of Count von Count, has died. One more.

In a box by his half-a-week bedroom, books my son has outgrown. Goodnight, moon. Moira says we should keep them.

In *Drowning by Numbers*, screenwriter/director Peter Greenaway wrote of the repetition of deaths: "Once you've counted a hundred, all the other hundreds are the same."

We refuse to allow the dead their rest. Respite. An urgency, as Greta Garbo's final possessions fall into auction, selling her intimate fragments, twenty-two years after her death.

Perhaps we never die. Perhaps this is the point.

6.

My grandfather, who carved pieces of wood into smaller, smooth pieces of wood. By the end, we were less sure what he was making.

Perhaps so in love with the form that results weren't as relevant. The hours he spent on the front porch.

Within his carved bubble, my grandmother called it.

Reading my late afternoon newspapers at the pub, I see the sweetest looking young woman in a floral-print dress stroll past the bay window. She is summertime, blissful. In her left hand, fresh broccoli.

7.

8.

A future in which, Lynn Crosbie writes in the *Globe and Mail*, people would die again and again, only to live forever. An elegant thought, excised from a longer quote.

Sesame Street, ad infinitum. Late-night Turner Classics, Garbo smiles, Garbo stares and Garbo laughs. Garbo withholds, for her protection.

At the coffee shop, the remains on the outside window of what I can only hope came from a spray bottle. What could be a sneeze.

The night of the August blue moon, Neil Armstrong's funeral. Later in the evening, a television commercial for memory foam, the effect of a right hand pressed into a mattress. Memory foam was invented, narration tells, after the first man walked on the moon.

Neil Armstrong, forever taking first steps on the dusty surface.

The world shapes itself to your absence.

On beauty

She knew the only way to prioritize was to record everything. She had to make a list. She wrote everything down,
constantly adding and shifting items. Put up the fence.
Get the roof fixed. Take the car in for maintenance. Snow
tires. Paint the walls of the nursery. All before the baby
arrived. As the list progressed, it became less a sequence
of tasks than a wish list. Catch up on reading. Meet up
with friends. Sort out the garage. By the time she'd
entered her third trimester, the list had become a bit
anxious, given how few entries had been completed and
crossed off. Sign up for swim lessons. Talk to father.
Travel. As she approached labour, the list had taken on an
abstract quality. Breathe more. Walk along the canal.
Notice the moon. As our firstborn began to crown, she
happened to glance up through the hospital window and
there was the moon, full and round and constant.

Things to do in airports

for Saskatchewan to appear for me again over the edge
horses led to the huge sky the weight and colour of it
    —*Fred Wah,* Medallions of Belief

1.
The mind seeks out patterns. The mind seeks out what is
familiar.

The ice cube slid from her left hand to the floor. She
blushed, and glanced around. An airport janitor,
replacing the bags in the garbage container at Gate D7
caught her eye, and smiled.

He offered: Let it melt. It's probably the cleanest thing on
the floor today.

This is how she imagined it. In reality, no one had noticed,
or commented. In the end, she realized it hadn't really
mattered. The ice had already begun to sink.

She suspected every airport was its own bubble, displaced
from the world. She suspected every one identical, in
design and shops, like so many suburban shopping malls.
A long way to travel to end up in the same location.

An ice cube, melting on the carpet of the Washington airport. She was between flights, from Toronto to Houston. She didn't know what was happening.

2.

Irina was unused to flying, wasn't used to airports at all. About to become a grandmother, and for the first time, lifted against the force of gravity. This was something unsettling, and deeply unnatural. When they first arrived in Canada, they'd come by steamer. Slow.

She feels displaced, as from the nineteenth century. A relic.

She coughs out recollections. Fills her aged lungs.

What was that poem she'd read? The "women of my mother's age," who survived beyond the burial of their husbands, babies. To see them now in singles, twos. Irina, herself, had long outlived her mother, far older than what she once considered ancient. Well after her mother had succumbed to dementia. Her whole self, folded.

This was where she lived, and had for some time: a woman of a certain age, no longer required to explain that her husband and son were dead. Only her daughter remained.

Irina envied her daughter. From a safe distance, of course. Sharp as a butcher's blade.

3.

Irina began to fidget, worse than a toddler. Delays. She
had abandoned the distraction of glossy magazines.
Patience was possible, but only had she known what she
was waiting for, and for exactly how long. This unknown
space of not knowing. An hour, or three.

In the airport, the security guards with assault rifles
unsettled her. Back home, it was an announcement of
families with small children who could board the planes
first, and others who required assistance. Here, the offer
includes military personnel. Irina wasn't expecting such
differences across borders, the shifting of values.

When her daughter was still home, they endlessly fought.
Once her husband died, and later, their son, the two
remaining bodies fell, and fell apart. Completely out of
orbit. They fell so far and so fast it was years before they
spoke. Irina alone in her grief, losing the whole of her
world in the short space of months.

But her daughter was sixteen by then. There was little a
mother could do.

4.

People, endless people. Even with infinite variety, most
of the crowd could be from anywhere, any city or country.
She people-watched, even as she ignored the endless
shops and kiosks, lineups for trinkets, postcards, sweat-
shirts and snacks.

Another hour, restless. The fleshy inside of her lungs,
coated in a fine dust.

Before the plane scheduled to board. She coughs, and
something catches, caught. Irina noticed the shift in the
air, recirculated. A dry, dull scent. Musty, slightly stale.

At the Washington airport, just across the state line,
this airport on the wrong side of the Potomac. She was
not in Washington at all. Through plate-glass windows,
she caught views of the White House, the Washington
Monument. The closest she'd come.

From her daughter's history courses, she was fully aware
of why their capitol had been painted white, whitewashed
to cover scorch marks, a northern response during the
War of 1812, to the American invasion and burning of the
city of York. She smiled, slightly. Coy.

5.
She nodded off, quietly. Slept.

The mind seeks out patterns, even where none might
exist. Irina, her head in the clouds. Lost. Was she safe in
her seat on the plane, or somewhere below?

Baby names

   ashless
are the voices
we have become
      —*Cole Swensen,* Gravesend

1.

Baby Iphigenia, shortened to If, and sometimes Iffy. She
was named for the leader of the Greek forces at Troy,
daughter of Agamemnon and Clytemnestra, who threw
her body down to save and solve her father's follies. Less
known than vain Helen, hers was not the face to launch a
thousand ships, but the sacrifice that prevented further
bloodshed. If only.

Names so often shortened. Names culled to their perfect,
familiar forms.

From the time she was a toddler, she held a certainty
that ignited calm in those around her, unable to discern a
single break or a crack. What not even water could unfold.

At twenty-eight years old, she knew her marriage was
over when she arrived late and later for appointments
with her husband. She knew he had done nothing wrong,
but they'd drifted apart, inch by restless inch. She didn't
even know she was unhappy until it came crashing in,

a single phrase from his lips, three glasses of another Okanagan red into waiting, again.

"Apparently it's 'If, not when,'" he added. There.

2.
Call me Ishmael, he said.

But that was not his name, and in the end, was not what we called him.

3.
Georgy Girl. Pregnant so very young, she named her baby daughter for the just-released Lynn Redgrave feature and the child grew to hate the association, opting instead for the full Georgina. She preferred, as she explained, a name with weight, something you could hold in your hand like a stone or a brick, not one you'd fear might float away. Her birth certificate was equally infected: Georgie.

Her mother thought the name sweet; Georgina associated it too closely with the awkward and unhappy film character. She'd had enough trouble of her own. She preferred the association with old King George, "Georgian," as was she. She delighted in the culture of this post-Edwardian period, rapt in King and Country, despite their home in the colonies. Nearly a century beyond, she flecked her hair with homemade fascinators. She scoured shops for antique hand-tatted lace.

The thread of the theme song, "Hey, there," outlined her childhood. Against her will it had imprinted deep upon her, from preschool lullaby her mother sang to school-yard taunt. When required, she learned early to punch, to throw, to knock down.

When she was twenty-three years old, she took the matter to the courts, and had her name legally altered— Georgina—and spent the following decade guilting her mother. The issue was resolved, but the injury would never fade.

4.

Since the turn of the century, new parents have worked through a sequence of names that those a decade or two prior knew only as "old lady names": Agnes, Myrtle, Charlotte, Laird, Ellen, Della. Names of women born a rough-century before, even earlier. With a gap of time, the old names renew, re-emerge. Quite literally, reborn.

In the 1980s, the gust of soap-opera Ashley and Kendra replaced the old standards of a Catherine, a Jane or a Jennifer. No family, it seemed, was immune. Names that return and replace any previous. Five girls in a grade school class with the same first name. Add or subtract their birth year times three, and the name is no less prevalent, yet entirely different.

Susan. Mina. Beatrice.

5.

Charles, as his father. Stephen, named for no one.
Identical twins, connected by a ten-second pause. As
Stephen felt rudderless to his brother's birthright, Charles,
as firstborn, envied his sibling's implied freedoms. Theirs
was a complicated relationship, a complicated fate, if one
might believe in such things. And yet, so simple.

Ten seconds between, and perhaps it never made a difference. Perhaps the differences were entirely artificial,
constructed. A seed they carved and cultivated, into the
divisions they became.

6.

So often, names help shape and announce identity,
chosen as arbitrarily as one might imagine.

The way my dairy farmer father named the new calves,
each year assigned a letter, alphabetical, to keep track of
their age.

Alice, Arlette, Annie each a year older than Bertha, Beth,
Bonnie.

In the file cabinet he kept in the milkhouse, paperwork
on every arrival, every animal he owned. A paperback of
baby names.

7.

As I had been adopted at ten months of age, my new parents changed my birth name into something that was meant to be entirely my own, if not theirs. The choice was under their discretion. Because of this, I have been me for most but not all of my life, uncertain how, or if, the shift has shaped me. Perhaps, instead, a rose by any other.

The Last Man on Earth

I entertain the pleasure of speaking out against
the heart of the material
   —Danielle LaFrance, Friendly + Fire

1.

After petitioning her parents for weeks, Verity was finally allowed an after-school visit to her friend Bekah's house. Once the final bell rang, the two girls strolled north to Bekah's finished basement, and sorted themselves with daytime talk shows, snacks and conversation. Two hours later, Verity emerged to venture alone to her scheduled bus stop, watching the minutes meander via her cellphone. Her bus appeared, she stepped on, and returned home.

Given Verity's solo jaunt had gone so well, it was easier to convince her mother to allow it again, and again. For Verity, the solitude of riding the bus was what she most enjoyed, nearly losing herself in the rattle and roll of mass transit. And, once seated on Alta Vista's #44 bus heading south, she has missed her stop only twice, forcing her to backtrack two blocks from where she should have landed.

Verity is twelve years old, and the freedom, even if but from singular point A to singular point B, is substantial.

2.

Bless or curse a man with daughters. As King George VI said of his two young girls: his pride and his joy. Elizabeth was his pride, and Margaret was his joy. What did that mean? It was an innocent enough remark, but one that also rendered young Elizabeth joyless, and Margaret's frivolity shameful. Was his oft-quoted comment a compliment, an insult, or a bit of both?

Home from preschool, Verity's sister Grace immediately abandons boots and socks in the living room. Their mother already in the kitchen sorting the day's mail, emptying the dishwasher, and collecting her dinner thoughts. Their mother a flurry of cupboards and movement. She broadcasts: Go play. Grace down the basement steps, television ablaze.

Verity in her living room chair, deep in a book. She won't come up for air.

3.

Oh so very Verity, her mother croons, during her morning sweep through the kitchen. Her mother is constantly in motion: coffee, toast, school lunches, iPhone. Verity, pausing her spoonful of cereal mid-scoop. Shush, mother. Shushy your mouth. This is issued so far beneath her breath it may as well have been buried. Her voice a lost river, covered in years of fill and veil. Whispers.

To Verity, her mother is rarely as clever as she reckons
but perhaps Verity is. As clever, I mean. A blind spot.

Whispering shush, a bowl full of mush.

4.
Verity is rereading a novel about a young prairie girl
who dreams of being an Olympic swimmer, a book rec-
ommended by her school librarian. It takes less than
an hour, but she rereads whole sections, attempting to
solidify some of the more abstract detail. She considers
the absence of the father, and the main character's insuf-
ferable pondering. She wonders how such a parental
absence might feel, and then feels guilty for speculating.

Mid-Saturday morning, her father most likely deep in
his weekend basement bunker, adrift in his projects.
Tinkering. What do we need, Verity wondered, with
another new lamp or Muskoka chair?

She slips back into her book. One of her frustrations
about her mother's iPad: the intangibility of turning
pages, forward or back. Days measured, as her father likes
to say, in dog ears.

What was that line from the movie, *The Hours*? She had
to die, so the rest of them could live.

5.

The freedom to fail. The freedom to try something new.
Verity's father realizes his daughters require, equally,
both. As appropriate. When Verity first started school, his
wife was far more nervous than he, but this is different.
This is her solo, out in the world. Her Red Riding Hood
innocence like a beacon to any lone wolf. It makes him
nervous.

In this, her father no more than a caricature. No more
than he requires.

6.

Verity was nine years old when they moved into this
house, shifting schools and friends for the sake of her
mother wishing for "space." The old house was too small,
her mother complained. What is the purpose of space? A
backyard they tend not to mow, or even use in the winter.
The front lawn maintained, and no more.

7.

As the seasons progress, Verity takes to remaining in
her seat two or three or four beyond her home bus stop,
striking a boundary past where her parents might have
expected her. She enjoys watching her house zoom past
the window, the grown-up-edness of rolling along with
end-of-day government workers and university students.
No one surrounding her knows where she lives, or which
stop is hers. Why does it matter? Each ride is a flourish, as

she spins up to the door and bounds down as graceful as butterflies, stepping outside to turn into the corner convenience for a snack before home.

This is freedom, she knows, of a sort. She tries not to abuse it, but neither would she wish to waste it.

8.
Verity, and her red-rimmed glasses, set to match her jacket. There are no accidents.

9.
What her aunt claims. Verity is so much like me at the same age. Another glass of wine.

Neither Verity nor her mother, for entirely different reasons, appreciate the comparison.

10.
Verity, in transit. Lately she's noticed the same man a few rows behind her, attempting her attention. Someone her father's age, thereabouts. Creepy, obviously. So creepy. He occasionally says hello, moves closer. Asks where she's headed.

She ignores him. She watches the houses and trees roll by along Alta Vista. The Shoppers Drug Mart.

This time: she steps off the bus at the correct stop.

11.

There have been newspaper articles lately about how
old or how young one is allowed to travel alone on public
transit. A divorced father from Vancouver who'd spent
an extended time training his four children to ride the
bus to and from school, only for a stranger to complain,
causing Children's Services to force them to suspend.
What should safety look like? When eleven-year-olds
are being trained via city-sponsored babysitting courses,
yet fifteen-year-olds can't ride the bus or cross the street
without supervision? When does safety turn into fear, or
absurdity?

12.

Two weeks later, returning home. The same man on the
same bus route. He attempts to force eye contact. Verity
rolls, turns away.

She wonders if she should pursue music lessons. Piano,
guitar. Her friend Lara plays harp, and two others, piano.
What are the benefits? Might her mother actually let her?

Where would they even get a piano?

Suddenly, the stranger shifts seats, appearing directly
beside her. She attempts to ignore him, but he's awfully
close.

Hand on her upper thigh. He smiles. Verity explodes.
FUCK OFF, she yells, directly at his face, at the top of her
lungs. He jumps back, startled. He looks around, frantic.
The bus slams to a stop.

On beauty

Before our son was born, we took classes. Multiple
classes. We watched videos, practised breathing and back
massage, spoke of bathtubs and yoga balls, folded diapers
in groups and practised CPR on baby dolls. Some things
can never be truly understood until you experience them.
In the end, her labour lasted thirty-seven hours. The midwife compared it to running five marathons. She was
exhausted. I was exhausted. Stunned as our newborn
pulled himself to the breast. Baby skin-to-skin as I quietly
wept, and our new trio drifted from anxiety to relief.

Art I have not made

A roller coaster is a series of problems on a steel track.
  —*Marie-Helene Bertino,* Safe as Houses

1.
Two free-standing, three-foot-tall rectangular containers
of transparent glass, built to scale of the former World
Trade Center towers. An opening left at the top of each,
and filled to the brim with water.

Fragile, so remarkably fragile. If we were to strike either,
you already know the result.

Am I documenting my failures or re-presenting them in
another form, writing them into existence? Writing them,
and therefore succeeding?

I am reminded of Leonardo da Vinci, sketching out the
impossible, which in his time, was only not possible yet.

I am organizing my sketches into files. I am organizing
my sketchbook.

2.
A short novel in four chapter-sections, each with its own
binding. Depending on the order in which the sections

are read, the story would shift, becoming something different. How to write a book that would allow such alternating perspectives? Perhaps a character dies in one chapter, perhaps in another the same character is seen strolling through a party by a semi-distracted guest. The story wants so much to be unstable. Just like you.

All my life, I have been attempting to uncover the connections between things. Attempting to comprehend, and articulate, whether chicken or egg.

When most authors autograph their books, I've noticed they scrape a small line across their name, printed there on the title page. What does this mean? Are they replacing their name with their signature? Is this a form of denial, instead?

Composing books is so personal, even the books that might seem otherwise. A biography of Sir John A. Macdonald, or *A Brief History of Time*.

Whenever I'm asked to autograph any of my works, it feels as meaningless and meaningful as signing my high school yearbook. I am seventeen years old. I want to write things like "You made gym class really fun," or "Have a great summer!"

I have no idea what to write. I don't know who you are.

3.

My travel novel from 1997, the small Canada Council grant I received to sketch out constant journals as I toured the country, six weeks east to west. Three notebooks to brim, I couldn't articulate a through-line, couldn't manage a text that cohered, scribbled page after page.

Hurricane Sandy, sea water pours into New York subway tunnels. Water and salt play havoc. City officials: Expect closures for weeks.

Once we have folded the river. An invisible seam.

I crept across prairies. Two days the train careened west, yet the hills inched no closer.

The Rocky Mountains would not come to me.

4.

A lifelong accumulation of twenty-five years on self-taught acoustic guitar, with, by the time I left home, the baker's dozen of years at weekly piano lessons. Somehow, songwriting is something that has managed to evade. The ongoing impossibility of performing publicly. The album I never made.

The one time I attempted to busk, hours on Rideau Street strumming Bruce Cockburn standards, resting legs on cold, concrete ground because I had no guitar strap. I couldn't recall any lyrics.

Failures are not failures, but opportunities. This is what I tell myself. I pilfer from notebooks, remove drafts from context, articulate the accident of reclaimed lines. I poem, slowly carve and expand.

Rhythms and lyric fragments disintegrate. Acoustic edge cuts into throat. I bleed, singing.

Beckett's oft-repeated phrase a mantra. Houston, we've had a problem.

Paul Simon, bouncing a rubber ball against brick backdrop for syncopation, a rhythm, brainstorming lyrics that slowly gain shape. I'm going to Graceland.

5.

In 2003, I apartment-sat a summer for a neighbour as he travelled, and worked his Gestetner, inviting writer friends over to each produce a single-page stencil. My aim was to curate, collate and create a small publication, instead of the half-dozen poems buried in a box, somewhere. Attempt to make at least one thing on every machine, someone once said, so I've tried.

The big-screen horserace, number six walks, shimmies sideways, kicks up, kicks. He will not stand still, will not

behave, even once the jockey is in position. Perhaps
something is wrong. Perhaps.

The shadows we fall across.

The earthquake off the west coast that temporarily dis-
abled a series of hot springs on Haida Gwaii. The springs
suddenly silent, cool and barren. Something shifted in the
plumbing. The hotel owners knew well enough to take a
zen approach; the only option was to wait, for what might
never come. The waters, well and calm.

6.

A novel in Polaroids: one hundred photographs, one to a
page, that accrue into a narrative. Handwritten text on
the footing of each, a story of a couple and one of their
friends. One hundred Polaroids, each image sculpted,
characters portrayed by actors, utilizing the uniqueness
of the quick click and outdated tech, blurred and half-
blurred snapshots that become the story.

A novel that progresses, develops, nearly as a box of dusty
pictures opened and read by a stranger. 1970s colour-tint.
Even my daughter now is old enough to remember the
company, before it came undone. A flood, of absence.

Now we have Instagram. One company thrives off the
corpse of another.

Sit down. I have a story to tell you.

A short film about my father

There is no such thing as fiction.
    —*Richard Froude,* The Passenger

1.
In 1968, my father and mother drive west along Highway
401, toward Upper Canada Village. They have been married less than a year. He wants to show her something.

This happens in real time. They drive.

Both his hands rest on burgundy steering wheel, his
cherry-red Ford. For the length of my memory, he owned
and drove only Fords: the family car and the truck for the
farm, upgrading every half decade.

The wind through the open driver's side window. His hair
so black it shone metallic blue. It sparkled. A trick of the
light.

2.
It begins with a silence, seeking its source. With occasional birdsong, the pant of the dog, a tractor rolling
along in the distance, the silence holds deep in its core.

We establish the fixed points: his daily routine, the pair of his and hers Fords in the yard, the black Labrador mix.

Much of my childhood was punctuated by silence. Inherited.

The silence remains, holding court amid tenor. At first, you might imagine it is waiting for something to be said, or to happen, but it is not.

3.

Their stretch of Ontario highway a madness of trees, awaiting development. Pitch-perfect birds and occasional deer. They pass farms and villages two centuries set. They drive west, into history. My father cities 1812 facts from half-remembered textbooks, mumbling dates and locations.

No, not awaiting. What's the word? *Dreading.*

They are newlyweds, still. My father rests his left arm across the ledge of rolled-down driver's side window. Air scrapes the length of his forearm.

My mother breathes deep, enjoys smokeless air.

4.

The quiet between these two is not absence, but slow comprehension. Each suspects what the other might say.

Years later, my mother would translate him, offering:
Your father is very angry at you for that thing that you did.

But for now, they are learning. They react to cues, whether
real or imaginary. They can't yet read each other's thoughts.

5.
We could speak of the father as imagined figure, since he
is not yet my father, or anyone's father, beside she who is
not yet anyone's mother.

We pause, on the obvious: their youth, their half-
restrained enthusiasms. One can't help but compare.
Baskets of apples and peaches, each nestled on the back-
seat. She is restless, flush. She has been wanting to
replenish their supply of preserves. Applied correctly,
wax seals freshness in.

Cellar shelves by the cistern. Fresh cobwebs and field mice.

6.
The seven villages along the St. Lawrence Seaway he witnessed, drowned through the Long Sault hydroelectric
project, during his mid-teens. Villages shifted, erased and
rewritten, for the sake of the water. Buildings broken, and
sold for parts.

A shed his father built from a former gas station, addi-
tions to the farmhouse made from what was once a single
family home.

The site of the Battle of Crysler's Farm, half underwater.
Inventing a pioneer village as a place-marker, upon the
remains. A shoreline redrawn by the flood.

They brought in buildings from across the area, including
half a dozen from a two-mile radius of my father's homestead. The cheese factory where his great-great-uncle
once worked, the one-room schoolhouse his own mother
and aunt attended.

We shuffle history around.

The house he was born in, a century old by the time he
was new.

7.
A marriage: two merge, inasmuch as they individually
change.

From the state of the farmhouse years later, it was as
though she married and left home with only the clothes
on her back. Her wedding dress asleep at the back of a
closet. She had little to nothing else pre-dating this, from
her homestead to his. What did she bring but herself?
What might she have left? What might she have meant to
bring, but somehow didn't?

A house sprinkled with archive: his rusted Meccano set,
his preschool plush lamb.

8.

In silent 1960s-era Super 8, colours are brighter, illumi-
nated. Nostalgia in luminous hues, glossy light. A quilt,
stitching squares of mere minutes. They drive. The
highway itself nearly new; less than two decades lain. So
close to the lip of St. Lawrence River, a sequence of edited
farmland and family estates scalpeled and shaped into
two and four lanes.

Their fathers are both still alive. His, living years with
cancer treatments, the three-hour drive into the city. My
father at the wheel, since my grandmother never learned.

He understands, distance.

He knows what lies across horizons, having crossed every
one.

9.

Her father, chain-smoking. The entire household. It
hovers around family portraits, Super 8 by the lake, where
they cottaged. My mother, once married, would never
light up again. She later frowned upon my own youthful
folly. Looked upon with derision.

Her once-mixed thoughts on the move, shifting city to
country mouse. Now she marvels at farmland, the open
green stretch.

Rewind. Leaving the farm, the truck kicks up dust from the gravel, two miles to blacktop. She twitches from crunch and the dust cloud, anew. Mixed thoughts, but this, she loved from the outset: a jolt to a small, giddy leap as they start up the laneway. A schoolgirl glee and excitement the city could never provide.

11.

My father, his hands on the steering wheel. The tan we now know as permanent. Melodic stretches of dirt road and gravel, of sonorous blacktop, that defy description.

From the Robert Creeley poem. Drive, she said.

On beauty

There is no such thing as safe. She skims posts from a variety of her Facebook groups, mothers posting notices on another dead child, another dead baby. One posts of their son who died a week prior, twenty-eight days old. A preemie, an infection entered his lungs, and he hadn't the strength to recover. Another memorializes the first anniversary of her daughter's accident, after toddler hands pulled a boiling pan from the stove, causing third-degree burns to thirty percent of her body. The scalding water had swollen closed her eyes.

When I walk into the family room, she is sitting with her laptop, weeping.

You need to stop reading those, I repeat.

The women appeared in the kitchen. They pushed me away from the counter. The lot of them. My mother-in-law and her sisters. Came rushing. They pushed me out into the living room. No, they said, no. They would take over from here. I had everything under control. I was annoyed, but not enough to challenge them. They had taken over. My newborn son and wife were asleep. I moved downstairs and sat at my desk. I ignored their clatter. I opened up my laptop and considered my most recent file. I poked at a few lines of prose. I prodded. The novel shuddered, some. Its surface tension shifted, akin to what Neo could see at the end of *The Matrix*. I could see stars.

Songs my mother taught me,

The failure of order is the work / disorder is not the work.
—*Phil Hall,* A Rural Pen

1.

Their mother claimed there were thirteen rules to live
by. Laird can never remember them all. If pushed, she
might be able to offer half a dozen, and rarely the same
list twice. "Don't take anything that isn't yours" is one she
consistently remembers. "Treat people the way you wish
to be treated."

"Always leave a place better than you found it."

She knows there are others. In all those years, no one had
thought to record them.

2.

Angus suspects there are exceptions to every rule.

The indignity of repeatedly having to explain to an in-
office barricade of federal middle-management that the
dictionary definition of *policy* is, in fact, "guideline."
Beyond the appearance of articulating power for its own
sake, nothing should be set in stone.

But this is government. After all.

He braces himself for another marathon session of meetings. He straightens his god-awful tie.

Given enough pressure and time, even stone can wear down.

3.

Raised on a farm, there were lessons she understood early: watch where you walk.

Now she misses little, nary a puddle nor mass of cow droppings, although in the city, the latter less likely. The occasional dog-drop. She might not have the poise her mother dreamed of, but she does have attention. She listens.

An ambulance spins on its heel at the corner, and screams through the lights. Across the street, a startled toddler gasps, and clutches her mother's hand.

Laird spots the copper glint of a coin on the sidewalk. Since the Canadian Mint discontinued pressing new pennies, and retail refuses them, they have become quite scarce. The penny-wish from a found coin might slip into history. More likely than adapting into a wish from a nickel, or dime.

Wishes are powerful things, and not to be trifled with.
Still, she decides to leave this particular wish for another.
She was already having a pretty good day, and life can
often be so very difficult.

4.

It was the third week of Movember, and already, a full
moustache down to the jawline. His fingers ran the
stretch of this new design.

Pink shirt and three-piece grey. All eyes turned to
follow as Angus strolled into the pub. He felt sharp.
Almost smug. He would make the air bleed. American
Thanksgiving, but he would catch the game from here.
As his mother would have called it: half a day's time and a
third of the effort.

Happy Thanksgiving, an American colleague emailed,
unaware the Canadian equivalent had long passed.

5.

After their mother died, the only request Angela had of
her siblings was that she be free to rescue the cookbooks.
It had been years since their mother had pulled down
her recipes, tucked away in the small cupboard above
the stove. Each binding rubbed down to dust and thread,
the pages waxy from age. When they were young, it was
through these volumes that their mother had instructed
the girls on the finer points of baking, fostering their

skills in lemon cookies, baked apples, and muffins constructed from the wild blueberries and raspberries that
flourished behind the house.

Their ancient mother: final sentry of the ancestral strong-
hold, nearly nine decades in that fading farmhouse. After
the funeral, the children, seven in all, collected themselves
in the homestead with cousins, spouses, partners and
offspring. Their mother's two remaining siblings. Each
adult cradling a glass of wine. She reached up to the cupboards to salvage. She wished, in her way, to become her.

6.

Around the time the first of her children arrived, Miranda
plucked from the vine of her grandmother's journals,
citing a list of precisely how one might live. She was old
enough to know there was wisdom in her grandmother's
lines, however brutal the woman herself might have been.
Spare the rod, indeed. She picked the fruit of her grandmother's knowledge, and adapted the list for herself. Her
MacDonald grandmother, who held on well into her nine-
ties, terrifying everyone around her; who read daily from
her own grandfather's Gaelic Bible, *Am Bìoball Gàidhlig*,
refusing to accept her scripture in English.

The closed palm, and the open fist. Lessons imparted
as cudgels, bludgeons with which to assault. Her grandmother, who wore mourning black for the forty-two years
of her widowhood. She wore it as an achievement.

The newspaper clippings of scripture, recipes and the occasional obituary.

Her grandmother, who saw the 1692 Massacre of Glencoe as a personal affront. She took every opportunity to pass insult along to her neighbours, the Campbells. You scurvy Lowlanders, she'd growl. You killed us in our beds.

Miranda adapted her grandmother's list, crafting a variation on twelve simple rules with an extra thrown in, for luck.

Christmas music

If it is true that the history of music has come to an end,
what is left of music? Silence?
  —*Milan Kundera,* The Book of Laughter and Forgetting

1.
Since realizing pregnancy, Moira declares: I am no longer
interested in fictional characters.

I want only what I can see, taste and touch, she says.
Moira has become increasingly tactile. Needles and pins.

At seven weeks, morning sickness less a crest and fall
than a permanent swell. She feels nauseous, nauseated,
most of the time. To throw up would be a relief.

It never comes.

2.
The minimum length of time before public announce-
ments is twelve weeks. At eight weeks, our midwife
presents baby's heartbeat. Twelve weeks, just short of the
differentiation of sex. Moira can't yet distinguish a boy or
a girl vibe.

A heartbeat, hummingbird, under her own. I have a
person inside me, she smiles.

Roots run, deep as the water-table. Strawberry plants, a
system of underground tendrils that burrow for miles.

Kilometre: when writing, I balk at the word. The metric
system might have entered Canada before I was born, but
we measured distance in miles; my mother her yardstick,
and so on. The word sounds too distant. My childhood
mapped out a world I have resistance updating.

I tap into black notebook: kilometres to go before we
sleep. Once the baby arrives, kilometres to go before we
ever sleep again.

3.

Something random and completely terrible happens.
Another school shooting in one of the eastern states.
Almost immediately, we attempt to ascribe meaning and
depth. We attempt to make sense of it. Is this simply a
question of faith, of a belief in a higher being, perhaps
God? Faith declares that everything happens for a reason.
Without that certainty of faith, some might fall apart, dissolve. Aimless. It can be frightening to have no ground
upon which to stand.

The entire idea of faith is believing in something that
can't be proven.

I catch a glimpse of the motorcade for the prime minister,
a row of black cars driving through New Edinburgh, into
Rockcliffe. I can't help but wonder: if our Conservative

prime minister looks and acts like a duck, for example. He moves like a dictator. The perception of fear, deliberately stitched between him and the populace. Bulletproof glass, in a country with but an occasional history of politically motivated violence.

The October Crisis. Paul Chartier. The Siege of Montreal, and the burning of York.

Idle No More, and a frustration building to a boil.

Years earlier, I met another prime minister while walking down Wellington Street, close enough to have done almost anything. But who was the last person who did anything?

I can't even remember.

4.

How to write of what is completely natural: the baby grows, sixteen weeks. We discuss names, unable to come to any agreement. Not yet having decided whether we will request to know the gender.

At our next scan: what does it matter? It might facilitate naming, focus our attention on a single shortlist, instead of two. The corners where our disagreements hold might be irrelevant. Think of the time we'd save, I suggest.

And waiting to be surprised: won't we be surprised either way?

Dandelion fluff. Hundreds of seedlings, following the eddies and gullies of air current over the trees. The air was thick.

A flock of white, intent with purpose, direction. Each one floating aimless, until a sweep of wind stream corrals and directs.

5.

From a newspaper photograph: Bobby Orr leaps sideways into the air, soars over the ice, celebrating an infamous goal. Recalculating.

When she selected a kitten from their local Humane Society, he came with digestive issues. The regular kitten food quickly replaced with more expensive bags of medicated kibble.

He can see right through you, she says. I find that difficult to swallow.

She says, I asked you to prepare dinner, not invent it.

6.

Twenty weeks. Offered the option of discovering gender, we accept. If baby decides to cooperate.

Everyone guesses: boy. How baby appears to rest, in the belly. We know the difference.

My father, his two slices of white bread, and bowl of maple syrup. One wipe.

In the beginning, there weren't even words.

7.

I can say it now: I hate Christmas music.

Veterans complain, suggest stores refrain further than the boundary of Hallowe'en, to the end of Remembrance Day. The feeling their day washed away in an annual yuletide commercial flood.

The trudge from mall entrance to the edge of the parking lot.

December snow, a mist. Coats the seams in the sidewalk, sweeps across car hoods, and catches in corners.

One must stand for something.

8.

Moira posts a photo to Twitter, via Instagram. She and her favourite aunt, a weekend in Fort Lauderdale, Florida, to prepare for what comes.

The southern heat applies pressure upon her chest. She has to remember to breathe. It does not come naturally. Air conditioning saves her. That, and virgin daiquiris.

We model our love on the unread book. There will always be another. It can't be enough. Our love is endless, boundless; held in boxes, on shelves, in stacks on the floor.

We are formed by our Canadian-ness, even if we don't follow the stereotypes. Hockey, maple syrup, Tim Hortons. I am indifferent to both hockey and winter, a child who preferred to remain indoors and survey the landscape from the safety of a window.

A dull grey sun over sparkling snow is still beautiful.

9.
Moira sleeps, unadorned. The cat wanders in. I navigate around, a wide berth.

News reports on the oil sands. If they could, they would monetize the air itself. What did the newspaper say?

The front of our car, absorbed into the snowbank. A light rain, coating all with a chill, and a layer of ice.

By dusk, it had learned how to sparkle. Reflecting the moon.

Moira's skin, always cold to the touch. Mine radiates heat. Sleepy, she reaches out.

On beauty

It is impossible to remain still. I can't remain still. I am a body in constant motion. Between baby, house, partner and writing, I am a body in constant motion, attempting two, three, four things simultaneously. I have always been capable at multi-tasking, but this is a new level. I bake as he sets down for lunch, and begin laundry and dishes as my wife attempts him down to sleep. I write an hour or two depending on the length and breadth of his nap.

I sketch a few lines in my notebook as he coos on his mat. Later on, I prepare dinner as they play together in the living room. Once dinner is made, set and sat, I prepare his bath and begin loading the dishwasher. As she watches him in the bath, I fold last night's laundry and diapers before assisting with bedtime routines.

Less than zero:
five imaginary stories,

Truth is impossible without an acknowledgment of noise.
  —Mark Truscott, Form

1.

With temperatures well below freezing, you watch as
a man walks briskly down the sidewalk wearing shorts
instead of pants. How could anyone, you wonder. It is
too cold, far too cold for exposed skin. The snow sweeps
gently in large, wet, accumulative flakes. Most disappear,
meeting blacktop.

The night prior, you picked up Chinese take-out, and
noticed the two women by the counter. They both wore
blue flip-flops, and you were baffled by their lack of proper
winter footwear. And then you noticed their brightly
painted toenails. This possible mother-and-grown-daughter
duo, the elder woman still with a trace of tissue paper
between toes.

An outing of pedicures, dinner. This made you smile:
their bond, and shared activity.

2.

Six years after your father dies, you make your way to
the back of the property, an unused five-acre patch of
Ontario bush. You played here as a boy; with memories of
summer days spent exploring corners and coulees, amid
footpaths overgrown by years. It was here you wished for
a treehouse or some kind of clubhouse, and your father
repeated, they aren't the right kind of trees.

You long suspected deflection. His white lie.

You spend days on and off tearing at trees and brush,
eventually working to scrape down to soil for pasture.
The property could always use more pasture. And then
you discover it, a row of stone set as a wall, perhaps a century abandoned. Not a wall between properties, but a
former structure. There are other clues too. You have no
idea how to read them.

3.

Instant karma, nineteen years old. This was the summer
you lived in Montreal on Queen Mary, spending late eve-
nings at Peel Pub downing pitchers of cheap draught beer.
Back before Foufounes Électriques, with its hard-edge
alternative club-vibe, added mini-putt gold to the outside
patch of gravel. Back when Dutchy's Record Cave existed,
and rare European pressings of big-name artists slid
out of plastic wrap, to be picked or even pilfered, by the
annual swell of September arrivals.

You won seventy-five pitchers of beer at a singing contest there, attempting to sing as the house band butchered familiar pop standards. Your only competition in the Lou Reed category: a man who screamed into the microphone. Given your natural baritone, the sound-alike competition was easily yours.

After three shared pitchers of draught before leaving, the certificate for seventy-two more was misplaced, long lost, and now there is nothing left but this recollection you can't prove to anyone.

4.

The story your father once told of a cow who'd escaped from the pasture. You realize this occurs, that cows are able to leap fences as well as horses, but rarely do, unless cornered. A childhood sprinkled with memories of the occasional escape, as farmhands and sometimes you, too, were corralled into a posse, circling to return wayward milk stock from cornfields, a neighbour's property, and even the front yard. What they'd do to the lawn, or your poor mother's garden.

Once that cow left it was never recaptured, quickly becoming a creature of local myth. For two years there were sightings, apocryphal tales, the impossibility of a domestic Holstein remaining free over the winter months in a mess of back fields, wooded areas and property boundaries. Every few weeks your father would receive yet another call to collect her, but she was not to be found.

5.

The first major snowfall of the season, and you already
know that by living downtown in a major centre, your
inconveniences are relatively minor. You walk twenty-
five minutes to work, and live a block from a main street.
At best, it's a waiting game.

The snow falls heavy, fast and full. The cat, anxious, chat-
ters at windows.

As your internet searches are calling it, this is a full-
blown snow day. School buses are cancelled, some schools
are closed, and certain government offices. The neighbour children are already outside, reshaping new snow
into structures, redesigning their backyard.

You wait half an hour before heading out. The snow
still comes, but the sidewalks and streets have been
plowed at least twice, and the walk may be slow, but not
treacherous.

When you land at the office at 9:30 a.m. instead of 8:45,
one-third of the seventh floor remains empty. By noon,
the lights flicker, and the whole building goes dark around
one. You are all sent home.

Translator's note

When the violin repeats what the piano has just played, it cannot make the same sounds and it can only approximate the same chords. It can, however, make recognizably the same "music," the same air. But it can do so only when it is as faithful to the self-logic of the violin as it is to the self-logic of the piano.

—John Ciardi, on translating Dante's Inferno *(1954)*

1.

This translation developed from my studies in Paris. For the stretch of my twenties and into my thirties, I was joyously self-entombed in the depths of the archives, poring through centuries' worth of manuscripts, diaries and journals. I wore gloves, and learned how to breathe. I learned the correct procedures for handling materials I couldn't have imagined accessing. I made increasingly detailed notes of what it was I read, and observed. I began a rolling list of words to search out.

For months I dreamed nightly of magical beasts, basked daily in the most intricate, and occasionally bawdy, illuminations. I caught images of lost saints and scribes in the clouds, and opened myself up to legacy, papal empires, pockets.

If I inhaled too deeply, I feared I might bite centuries into my lungs, smothered by what I had hoped might enlighten.

A trail of high school Spanish to Portuguese, circling back to Old English.

Is the role of translator to explain, to reveal, or to assert dominance? To make cleaner, more relevant, more modern? One attempts to step aside, and let the words reveal themselves.

To paraphrase Auden: We survive in the valley of our making.

2.
I nested in those archives. Sketched out variations on what it was I thought I was reading, and how best to artic-ulate the text into a thoroughly modern language.

By my third year in Paris, I'd begun a relationship with one of my professors. She told me I had lovely eyes and the longest eyelashes she'd seen. She was born and raised in Berlin, and spoke English with a pronounced German accent. Every statement implied a command.

There are stories I've told too often, and others I might never tell. That night we spent under the stars in Born, or the game at Wrigley Field where I caught a foul ball and broke three fingers on my right hand. Her first bout of pneumonia, as we sat up all night in emergency. She told me stories of her own, and I told her about the time our dog lost a leg, the next few years around the fields still fast as anything.

The way her father strummed fingers on surfaces when he was nervous. The unfathomable distances that would occasionally be revealed behind her mother's eyes. Those unbearably sad eyes.

Those frantic first weeks of our new romance, sneaking around campus and through back staircases, hallways, into her office. We assumed ourselves quite invisible, unaware how much and how quickly an open secret we already were, throughout the department.

Twenty years later, I held her hand and sang from her mother's catalogue of folk songs. As she lay dying. As the cancer slowly took her, from me, and from her new partner, who appeared soon after I'd left.

Perhaps a particular window passed, and interest in the authors whose work I'd been translating faded. My own fault, I suppose. I had more than enough time to peak before that happened. Enough time to speak.

3.
I have recurring X-rated dreams. I should speak no more of this.

I should not charge against that which I cannot hope to conquer.

4.

When I was young, I would regularly imagine the worst possible scenarios, ones involving the violent deaths of my partner, parents, friends. Car accidents, home invasions and even zombies. Once I imagined a post-apocalypse in which I remained the sole survivor of our neighbourhood, fearing attacks from roving bands of scavengers. How would I barricade myself in the house? What would I do for food, and for how long?

It had become a coping mechanism. A strategy, meant to reduce my ongoing anxiety. If I had already imagined the worst, then regular life might no longer frighten me.

Splitting hairs: did I live in or within fear, or against it?

5.

My years of envy of the British Isles, and Europe generally: the immediacy of their lengthy histories.

All I achieve with this admission is a broadcast of privilege, and lack of knowledge: just how much I remain ignorant of the landscape of my own upbringing. The shores of Lake Ontario, and the thousands of years of Indigenous occupancy. A shame that our country and culture has yet to rectify. And myself, it would seem.

During one of my explorations of the British countryside, a man from the village told me the story of a particular medieval king: he rode down this road right here, and turned down the lane, where he met the enemy in battle. And then he pointed past his elder brother's house, a house that had remained in their family for generations. More than they had thought to count.

The story itself, eight hundred years old, and backed by historical record. Handed down locally, throughout centuries. The road and the lane remained, as did the field. As though it could happen again, at any moment.

Back home, someone finally listened to the stories told by Inuit, and "discovered" the ruins of Sir John Franklin's lost expedition, the HMS *Erebus* and HMS *Terror*, some one hundred and seventy years after they had been lost. They had been searching for years for what the locals had long known the location of. The remains of the *Terror* resting in, appropriately enough, Terror Bay.

6.
A good plumber doesn't blame his tools.

Alec Baldwin on *Inside the Actors Studio*: an actor's job is to do the work. When you hire a plumber, his job isn't to respond: I wouldn't *dream* of putting a sink there.

In his essay "The Art of Translation," Vladimir Nabokov banishes to hell "...the translator who intentionally skips

words or passages that he does not bother to understand
or that might seem obscure or obscene to vaguely imagined readers; he accepts the blank look that his dictionary
gives him without any qualms; or subjects scholarship
to primness: he is as ready to know less than the author
as he is to think he knows better. The third, and worst,
degree of turpitude is reached when a masterpiece is
planished and patted into such a shape, vilely beautified
in such a fashion as to conform to the notions and preju-
dices of a given public. This is a crime, to be punished by
the stocks as plagiarists were in the shoebuckle days."

An art known not by what it knows, but by what it tries to
seek out.

7.
In Paris, she chastised me for my Union Jack tee. How
can you wear that here? And she was only half-joking.

The problems of empire. One can still love something
that is imperfect. One can still love and wish to argue, and
disagree.

She thought me naïve. If you want to admire a country,
admire Afghanistan, able to hold off the most powerful
armies of the past century: England, Russia, America.

Paris, where the word *bistro* emerged from the Russian
word for "quickly," from the 1814 Russian occupation.
How can you not know this, she asked.

8.

I am shaped by these words, as I understand them. As I
have, through research, experience, and study, decided to
understand them. Even as any good translator lets themselves become immersed in a particular work or body of
work, that too is a choice. I have chosen this, as my translation of this particular work.

9.

On National Boyfriend Day, @adultmomband posted:
"that ex u still romanticize is just a concocted projection
based off of everything they never were able to give you."

All of this is projection. All of this is created.

I may have no words of my own.

Opening

The house where I was born no longer exists, not that it
matters, because I have no memory of having lived in it.
   —*José Saramago,* Small Memories: A Memoir

1.
She had fallen asleep in her chair in the kitchen. She
awoke to her caramel-coloured tea ice-cold, a trace of
half-eaten toast. The kitten bookmark her daughter had
gifted for Mother's Day, slipped into her Agatha Christie.

From a cardboard box in the sewing room, paperbacks
she regularly pulled to read and reread.

She preferred a good mystery, but found it more com-
forting to know how it ends. She rereads for clarity, to
understand how the story arrived.

2.
She awoke to a rustling, the sound of the door separating
kitchen and covered front porch. Her husband, perhaps, returning from his work in the yard. She awoke in
her armchair, with notepad and pen on her lap. The television remained on, showing a sequence of images from
London, camera snaking through Roman-era drainage.
The sewers.

He came in to speak to her. Half-awake, she caught only
fragments. Wait. A neighbour has died. Their immediate
neighbour, found in his driveway some two hours earlier,
dead from a heart attack.

The funeral is most likely Thursday, with the wake
Wednesday night. So she knows.

This neighbour, but six years her elder.

3.

Prioritize rest, her doctor repeated. Don't overdo. The
metal chassis that rode a binary rail between floors: five
meditative minutes per ride. If she could make it.

4.

She awoke in her chair, crossing midnight. The news. Her
husband, who'd retired three hours prior. She rose to a
series of aches and stiff joints. Slow.

Tea, and blank toast. Go, lightly. Before heading to bed,
she required food to chase a mélange of late pills. Their
black Labrador, too, sniffed for her share. A slip of toast.
The two, making night of their rituals.

5.

She awoke amid hospital linens, and the pink colour of
dawn. High above, the flutter of helicopter blades displaced air. The sound startled her, the advent of yet
another emergency.

Her thirty-first consecutive hospital morning, with IV tube in left arm, held by plastic-thick tape to the back of her hand, needle puncture, seeking the vein. Separate line to her chest. Even for the unconscious body, tubes restrict certain mobility. The body remembers pain, and how best to avoid it. She awoke in the same position she'd fallen asleep.

The nurses pad from room to room to their station.

She drifts back to sleep again, slowly. She drifts, floating. She is a clear glass bottle with note inside, bobbing atop waves, unmoored. The perspectiveless horizon in a near-endless ocean.

On beauty

I wonder if it is possible to compose my biography solely
through the objects that surround me. I wonder what
kind of portrait this might present. Meaning so often gets
stripped away the moment I am removed from the equa-
tion. It just won't add up. Books and toys and trinkets and
photos and small items rich with personal histories and
consequence, unknown to anyone else. Must I annotate
my office for the sake of posterity? It sounds like non-
sense, but then. Twitter asks, what are you watching? I
haven't an answer.

The Gospel According to Portia,

To underline one passage is to help you locate it again
   —Phil Hall, Notes from Gethsemani

1.
Held in place. Portia. A customer places a right palm on
Portia's belly and smiles. Perhaps the woman assumes
there is something there, something new. Portia pauses,
startled. Arms wrap around menus, electrical impulse.
She shows them their seats.

   There is nothing there. There will be no more.

There would be miracles. There would be none.

2.
This is shaped like an argument. Some tales never
survive.

Whatever they were doing, had been only four months.

3.
Portia, her porcelain pallor. Not a black hair out of place.

It had been the warmest of summers. From June onwards,
Portia stepped mornings out her front door, and watched
as the steam rose from bare skin.

Flush-drunk. Right foot on pavement, a world of heat-
waves, exhaust fumes, and this.

4.

They met for drinks that summer, every few weeks.
Rarely planned, casual, last minute. Let's have a drink,
one would text the other. And they would, have drinks
and conversation. The books they had read, what movies
had held them down deep in the soul.

Her vodka and soda versus his pints of lager.

At the end of each session, she'd invite him back home.

5.

Portia had known for some time, if she had any super-
power, it would be through will. Her powers increased
with resolve. In her brother's stack of *X-Men* issues, she
found her doppelgänger: Gladiator.

But if she'd her druthers, she'd be Iceman, changing
shape, to melt under locked doors, slip down and up
ice slides. She's better as Gladiator, leader of the Shi'ar
Imperial Guard. Her confidence makes her strong.

6.

What does the body know but of itself? A wonderment
of limbs.

Portia, in portions.

The third time, she rolled over a morning, and spoke out loud. I like you, she said, but you're too annoying to date.

7.
Devil with a blue dress on, he sang. She scowled. They dismantled the awning.

During the day, she sang songs to herself, off the top of her head. Once, when you and I were nothing.

8.
Across the urban park, a fragment of city block, her toddler breaks the sound barrier. Portia hears only a blue, sudden noise as he clambers up red-painted ladder.

He strikes sneaker heels against metal slide, gleeful. Turns to wait at the top, he searches for her.

9.
She became pregnant quickly. Almost too quick. She felt the difference at the moment of conception.
    Her sudden shock at herself, asking: What did you do?

Fearless

A plane is standing still in
the air above the skyscrapers
    —*Emmanuel Hocquard,* Conditions of Light
        (trans. Jean-Jacques Poucel)

1.
A shared experience does not necessarily mean a shared response.

His mother still a child the day John F. Kennedy was assassinated. That terrible afternoon in Dallas, the news broadcast worldwide. The headmistress entered each classroom in turn to announce to the students and faculty. They thought the whole world might end. Several girls in her math class started to cry.

A shared moment, but what does that mean? No shared knowledge, empathy or comprehension. As many potential versions as observers, multiplied exponentially through the tellings.

Layton Hunt is attempting perspective.

An airplane whispers above, flickers silver-grey.

2.

What startled him most were the airplanes. Passenger
jetliners, threading the air above Capital for the length of
his memory.

Look, Layton, an airplane, his mother trilled. She
stared into baby blue, directing his preschool gaze to a
scalpel of bleeding exhaust.

Four days after 9/11. Such an absence.

What the planes had become. Just what they had done.

3.

His mother relishes the retelling, of the time she was
arrested soon after they first arrived, discovering that
they were unable to enjoy wine in movie theatres. She
was aghast. She still is. What kind of provincial backwater
had she been forced to?

Sunday dinners, surrounded by family.

The ends of the Château Rayas. Another dead soldier.
As she turns to retrieve another, she requests he set the
empty bottle by the back door.

4.

Layton finds comfort in knowing exactly where his feet
are at all times.

Ten years old, he pondered the opposite edge of the
creek as his friends called out: Jump, Layton, jump. Take

a running start. He refused. One foot on the ground before a foot in the water and the first foot in the same water.

He took no uncertain steps. Not a one.

5.

Layton had been in love, once. A long time ago.
    Time passes like this for reasons we don't understand.
    Rarely is anyone suddenly in and then out of love.
More often than not, it ignites, burns solid, and is consumed.

By the time they'd severed, she was already past tense.

6.

His wife tells the waitress he favours merlot. Layton can barely distinguish wine by colour. The deep reds he prefers, or the clear white swirls that send spikes through his frontal lobe. It was something to do with the sugars.

On television, there is a fire.

When he was in his early teens, he witnessed the live feed of space shuttle *Challenger* lifting into Florida sky. At first he did not understand. What just happened? It wasn't until the camera panned the crowd of astronauts' families, agitated, stunned. Unable to fully react. The absolute horror of what had occurred.

7.

Layton wants to know. Layton demands.

On the Greyhound bus between Calgary and Banff, he
read an article in *The Walrus* on how songs considered sad or depressing are, in fact, uplifting. We release
our negative feelings and energies through hearing sad
music. Once released, how darker feelings are less likely
to impact.

His uncle, a retired civil servant in Ottawa, whispers: If
you want to have an affair, don't bother in Ottawa. It's a
small town. A million people, but it feels like a hundred
thousand. If you have an affair here, you're screwed.

8.

There is an airplane, absent from the horizon. Nothing
lifts, or sets. It makes all the difference.

Charles Lindbergh, who lifted from tarmac and yet, his
infant son was the one who disappeared. Unsolved. The
Lindberghs, distraught.

Amelia Earhart, who once trained as a nurse's aide in
Toronto, where she first caught the impulse of flight. The
small fabric scraps in the silt of a South Seas island.

To rise into the air and vanish. Dissolve. Or to finally
descend.

On beauty

Toddler negotiates the coffee table against a backdrop of bookcases. The lowest two shelves are protected by baby-gate; not as a barrier constructed between spaces, but to guard the volumes themselves. He pulls books. A post-card, business card or press release might slip to the floor. A cover might tear. We do this to protect our collection, protect ourselves from the stress and worry of damaged or misplaced titles. You might ask, why have so many? We have books, and new titles arrive daily. One upon one upon one. It is a system of weeks before stacks from the desk absorb into shelves. We attempt a small sense of order. By author, the books are alphabetized by letter but not yet within each letter. *Sm* beside *Sa* beside *Sl* beside *Sp.* There isn't the time. With small children, one might consider the shelves alone quite the accomplishment. One might just be right.

In all of this, there is barely a chance to breathe. To breathe. There is no such thing as a chance to breathe. I haven't a moment. I am always in motion.

He is constantly in motion. I remember thinking, also: I am always in motion.

Silence

Books themselves take time, more time than most of us are used to giving them.
  —Ali Smith, Artful

1.
I awoke from a dream of fire. In my dream, I was standing alone in our two-bedroom condo, which morphed into a three-storey Victorian house. The flame was deep. The air sparked.

White curtains shrivelled. The pulse of my footprints burned into the hardwood.

The fire surrounded me, feral, and grew. It concurrently curtsied, swung, screamed running, jumped bare-boned and stood, stock-still.

I wake, woke, startled. A confusion of tenses. Bedsheets damp at my chest and my belly, smelling of sweat-musk.

Asleep on my left side, I pushed slightly back, jostling against him just enough to hear him grumble, feel his slight shift of torso. Make room.

We settled, both of us, and melted, returned immediately to sleep.

2.

I don't know anything about you.

At thirteen years old, she salvaged three books of matches
her mother had abandoned on the kitchen counter. Each
held a busty outline with neon lettering, plucked from her
father's laundry.

From the back step she caught the firefly of passing
headlights sprinkle up from the highway, through
summer dark. The evening settled, inch by noticeable
inch. She flicked matches, lit, at the moon.

The moon rose, orange-pink. She did not know the
name of it. She did not know that each moon had a name.
Pink, Wolf, Harvest. Errant Blue.

The breeze stole the last of the matches and flung it,
mid-air, into a stack of cardboard, set resting against the
house. Before she could recover it, flame began to devour.
Cardboard refuse smouldering slow from the inside. It
took. Burning cardboard, up against brick.

She panicked. She stomped with her feet and mashed
the worst of it out and the rest in succession, ash floating
free in small gusts. Like black butterflies.

3.

What is often most important is what is the most mun-
dane. The jars beneath the kitchen sink. The coupons
that created her stockpile. Dish soap, laundry detergent,
toothpaste, cereals, tissue and toilet paper, diapers, wipes,

crackers and salad dressings. This is what has kept us, she knows. What stretched them beyond their small incomes. It had helped make them strong.

Her father's only advice: Never pay full price for anything.

She clipped and saved, negotiating the spaces between the world, between commerce and income.

Couponista, she called herself. It was more soothing, even impish, compared to what her husband had named her: crazy coupon lady.

4.

I woke from a dream, which was a dream of fire. My skin was warm, and yet, would not burn. I was hot metal naked, deep through the conflagration. Not a hair on my body was singed.

In the mirror, I could see only what fire had left.

It flickered deep inside me. I felt the flame harden blue, low in my abdomen, resting just on the bladder. The baby kicked, and I became agitated. I feared for my baby, trapped inside with the fire. I clawed at my belly with hands and fingernails, finding little but blood.

And then I stopped, realizing that the baby wasn't trapped inside with the fire. He was the fire.

My skin froze. Water vapour rose from the surface.

And I was afraid.

5.

According to stories, what Gilles de Montmorency-Laval, Baron de Rais, caught first was the smell. It was May 1431, and he had arrived too late to save the maid, Joan, from her death at the stake.

The skin blisters, bubbles, burns. Skin blackens, fades and crumbles.

The sight of my old flame: a meaning that didn't emerge until far later, into the 1840s.

Joan, burning up into fable, and legend. Cremated, burned alive. De Rais arrived too late, and spent subsequent years killing and burning the bodies of young boys and girls, releasing the scent of burnt flesh. He might have killed hundreds.

He, who has been falsely identified as the model for Bluebeard.

He killed, savagely. By recreating the loss, he had also recreated the moment immediately preceding that loss, when a life with his near-lover Joan was still possible. He burned.

Is this love turned impossibly ugly, or a form of pure narcissism?

Whatever might have been beautiful in him had been broken.

6.

I don't think I am afraid of my unborn child. A flutter, evolved into a kick. The sensation is impossible to describe, but for what is obvious: the feeling of being struck from the inside.

I dream cannibal dreams. Sometimes I am ravenous, violently attacking everyone around me, and feeding off the remains. Sometimes I am the one being consumed, from the inside. Like some dark version of Victorian consumption, a cough bleeding into white linen. To waste away in a sigh, the back of my right hand affixed to my forehead.

I am afraid of what I do not yet know. I am afraid of fire. This soft, growing flesh within coincides with but one of those fears.

Most days I am certain which one, but other days, I am not.

7.

It is not uncommon for pregnant women to dream of being devoured.

Geena Davis in *The Fly* and her nightmare of giving birth to larvae, the result of her husband's terrible metamorphosis.

They say to know a person is to read what they've written. I write in my journal, daily. I wonder what it might say about me.

There is a lonely teenage boy in every pop song.

8.

The way you can see heat, in the air outside, shimmer. My father, who once melted vinyl siding along one side of the homestead, unaware of the potential heat generated from the back of his barbecue.

From my third-storey vantage point, a sequence of neighbourhood cats skulk about, each with its own shady purpose. I stand on this Saturday afternoon deck, while in the yard behind ours, small children scream in turn on their swing set.

I am learning to filter out everything.

This is how it happens,

In every part of every living thing
is stuff that once was rock
—Lorine Niedecker, "Lake Superior"

1.
In the opening of Charles-France Landry's great
Canadian novel, *Precipice*, he describes the unnamed
mountain as a finger. The novel opens, voice-over, to a
filmic panorama: the blue-eyed British Columbia peaks,
winking snow-capped scrape a tear, and every tear, a tear-
drop, shaped in cloud.

   She knows the book so well, she has memorized the
pages. She has started to read between them.

2.
In her final year of high school, Juliet adapted a fraction
of a short story she loved into a three-minute monologue. Ezra Pound confined in his cage near the end of
the Second World War, animal-frenzied in an American
internment camp just north of Pisa, Italy. Timothy
Findley's "Daybreak at Pisa." Learning by tone, and by
heart, and the way she stood on the stage—feet slightly
apart, braced for a blow. She held and hunched, pulled
up the collar on her thrift-store overcoat to become him.
Beneath her breath, she cursed.

She hunched, hunkered, lumbered. She lunged across the stage. Shallow breath, to quicken anxiety. In her best caged-animal tone, she let fly the opening line as accusation, stretching skyward: Where are the birds?

3.
She read through the novel, again. She sketched out her notes, which began to form their own shapes.

She had a passion for fiction, but anything too lengthy bored her, and anything too short, unsettled. Everything about this unsettled. As Pound himself wrote: Beauty is difficult.

At night, she dreamed of 1940s-era film stars. She wished her surname Lake, like Veronica. Have you been to the shores of Veronica Lake? She imagined: Veronica Lake Arms, resting on a charming hill overlooking the beach.

In daydreams she stands barefoot in the sand of Veronica Lake Beach, staring straight out into the depth and breadth of the water. Sun transforms the surface to silver.

4.
In the fire, charcoal replaces wood. Wood, from peat. On the barbecue, she turns the venison with tongs.

In her small cottage, electric heat replaces fire. In the distance, the hum of a chainsaw. The hum becomes purr.

Her dissertation accepted, defended, fades into history.
She writes, freely. Deep lines of prose. Impossible depths.
If she were to suddenly rise, air bubbles quick in her
veins. She might burst.

5.

Her dissertation: the scrapbooks of Catharine Parr Traill.
Upper Canada during the Victorian era, sister to Susanna
Moodie, roughing it long in her Lakefield wild. Two
Strickland sisters from London who both married the
backwoods, and emerged, pioneers.

Traill, who composed scrapbooks as personal gifts for
family and friends. Of dried wildflowers, maple leaves
and clippings from Stony Lake, gathered, mounted and
annotated. Scrapbooks built for a nephew, a neighbour,
a grandson. Companion grasses, collected. Traill, who
studied and sketched out her breadcrumbs, dark commu-
niqués sent from a bottomless wilderness.

Juliet saw echoes in the ritual from other British con-
structions, from Victorian gardens to the museum of
curiosities. A controlled, tamed wilderness; a domestic
bliss from the formerly savage. A collection of lions in
pens, fangs filed or pulled.

6.

It was the only book he wrote. Charles-France Landry,
late Victorian and early Edwardian lawyer, banished to

the colonies as penance for some unrecorded, unheralded
crime. Some thought a possible murder, others suspected
a dalliance with a married socialite. They weren't even his
colonies, but he was sent, nonetheless. He attempted to
practise in these lands his grandfather might have known
as Lower Canada for fifteen years, before disappearing
into the hills.

Letters home recorded his erosion: Quebec City is not
Lyon, and I could not be further from the truth. This city
is a lie of civilization in the unforgiving wilderness.

Toronto suffered far worse: an ugly mud-pit, that could
only be redeemed through cleansing fire.

Ottawa, the capital, was not mentioned.

7.
Juliet. All she knew was the book. All that she knows.

She placed her hands on the manuscript. Long fingers,
white and bone-thin. Her grandmother's hands. What
else they share: the red ruby keepsake on left ring finger.
    Something her father once said about his mother's fin-
gers: they were always so quick to grab at his arm, to wrap
themselves like ribbons around the leather strap.
    Unspooled, it remained a confusing image. She consid-
ered brightly coloured ribbon wrapped tight around dark
leather.

In Sanskrit, *anamika*, the name of the left hand's fourth finger. Which translates to "nameless." *Sanskrit* itself, a word that means refined, adorned, well constructed or completely formed.

She no longer recalled her grandmother's name.

8.

Precipice: whether something to leap from or into.

It was in these dark woods where Landry's novel was birthed. Emerged, and remained. A manuscript in Juliet's hands, slipped into a metal box and forgotten. It is hers, alone.

Some write to discover, some write to find themselves, and others to disappear. Landry, unmarried. The missives sent over God's endless ocean to his dwindling family, registering his list of complaints and contusions, his near-endless wounds. He was a man banished, in exile. Eroded, to the point of erasure. There was nothing to find. All that remained, in the pages of a single manuscript, tucked into a crevice of a dusty cabin.

After an unknown scope of years had passed, the cabin had been presumed abandoned, and sold. Disappeared. Juliet's father and grandfather. Juliet, her small hands reaching into the darkness to where the body lay, in the space of these pages.

9.

The remains of stone hearth in the bush was a mystery,
one she felt no urgency to solve. To solve every riddle
would be to reduce the magic of the world. On sunny days,
she would sometimes wander there to sit quiet and think,
and occasionally catch the curled clip of the red-winged
blackbird.

There were birds she knew the names of, some she didn't
yet. The sparrow, starling, cardinal. A mathematics of
small birds, scattered across the acreage. She rolls out a
litany of facts and names, her personal rosary.

I am Elliott Gould in Robert Altman's *The Long Goodbye*,
Juliet said, to no one. I am Philip Marlowe.

All at once, she had no destination. Her grandfather and
her father, the clenched fist and the open palm.

It was the only book he wrote. Somewhere toward the
end, someone says, all books are exactly the same. He had
to write only one.

On beauty

I float through Facebook, skimming the links. An article suggests that writing begins with forgiveness. What is there to forgive? A vague selfishness to even attempt something that, at least on the surface, isn't useful for anyone. A friend over coffee tells me that this is an impulse women writers are far too familiar with: the guilt associated with writing, when one should instead be caring for a partner, for children, for anyone other than themselves. She says that the pressures upon the female writer are far worse. *Can my attempt to write in fact harm his work?* She knows full well that such feelings aren't reasonable, and yet, there they are. This has the potential to self-fulfill, even as the male writer worries not just about his own work but hers. So much energy is wasted on the wrong things.

Am I doing the work I am supposed to be doing? Time at my desk relegated to distraction, deflection or housekeeping. Is this what I want? Am I seeking a life in which one sacrifices for the sake of the work, reduced to producing work of so little volume or quality, and even less consequence? As that manuscript lies unfinished, will a dusted bookshelf matter, or might it just be the end of me?

A bumper sticker reads: Jesus Is Coming! Look Busy.

The New House

Because I am full of love, I am full of sorrow.
  —*Kristjana Gunnars,* The Prowler

1.

From here you can reference endings, beginnings, and all in-between. We had accepted the counteroffer, four days of a back-and-forth that continued to put us on edge. What if someone else had stepped in during that period, turning our attempt to reduce the price into a bidding war? What if, after forty or fifty viewings, we were forced to continue looking? We had already come home. Both girls in their sketchbooks, in the process of picking, sorting, and designing their bedrooms.

2.

Here, we do not discuss my father: he withered, as the cancer replaced him. My father, a dried shell: focusing his personality into a pinprick. He'd been always a prick, my wife countered. A needle, driven deep into the hearts of whoever came close.

A mistake rarely repeated. There were always exceptions.

My cancer-father, the lepidopterist. His family and friends reduced to a sequence of pinned insects. A shadow-box, butterflied.

3.

During hospital stretches, chemo burned through his
layers. I sat mute, reading *Don Quixote*. I read in patches,
more often rereading. Sections that would not absorb.

The hospital smelled of pennies, burnished steel. Of blood.
Incrementally beige. Technologies tear us to pieces. My
father, who raged into deflation. There was no air for him
left to breathe.

My greatest achievement: my failure to properly read
Don Quixote.
    Failure, perhaps, being all I required.

4.

As a teenager, I raged, and I raged. We, each, a mirror.
Then my best friend's father introduced me to the game
of golf, slow putts in the backyard of their suburban
duplex. A singular, meditative sport. A game of scotch and
poems that rhyme may have saved my stupid life. I began
to dream of languid greens, and small white specks that
disappear in baby blue.

Perhaps it is impossible to know.

5.

My grandfather, who, over the course of five decades, won
and lost enormous fortunes.
    A curious pleasure inherent to the telling of old stories.
With each subsequent exchange, the story modifies,

refuses to remain static. Neither, storyteller. To say, you cannot step into the same river.

After reading his biography, I am rereading a novel by Richard Brautigan. The novel, too, has changed.

6.

Homeowners. We tear at the topsoil, attempt to correct the exterior grading, touch up mouldings, add new gutters along the boundaries of a roof that will require eventual replacement. We feel terrified, grown up, abandoned. Switching from renters to owners, my wife and her binder of house-related mathematics, from mortgage to water bill to property taxes.

7.

The difference between renting and owning: a series of phone calls, an interruption of work, and an outlay of cash. Handyman, eavestrough company, foundation guy, plumber. The woman who helped replace oil with gas. She had large hands, a kind smile and a practical eye. Proudly introduced digital snaps of her toddler.

8.

I abandoned *Don Quixote*. I could not even keep up with failure. I began to see ghosts, staring through my periphery. An anxious exhaustion, both physical and emotional.

God draws out his plans, Sheila says, attempting a comfort. I don't know what to believe.

When the girls were born, my father laughed. Twins,
he said. It's almost enough for me to believe in a higher
being. Someone is obviously punishing you. He wouldn't
refer to them again.

9.
Misery might love company, and in many ways, he was a
company man. Since the death of my mother, he simply
folded. He became untenable.

Without her as life raft, he became fully submerged, deep
into anger.

And yet, with the final accounting of his estate, and I
his only remaining relative, an unexpected generosity.
Enough to allow a considerable down payment for a
three-bedroom bungalow.

We required the space. But still. There is no reconciliation.

Can I allow this as a gift, a parting?

A dream about vegetable soup

when memory attacks

bring breath back
one thousand times
   —Stacy Szymaszek, austerity measures

1.

When she informed him that she had accumulated a list
of names, he assumed it had been exclusively created for
potential future offspring, and immediately felt uncomfortable. Only you could see a list as threatening, she said.
Originally compiled when she was thirteen years old, her
collection had been copied and adapted through twenty
subsequent years of bound notebooks: as new names
added, others removed. Created not exclusively for possible children, but for the names themselves.

Moira had long been fascinated by names, and how we fit
into them. How could anyone manage to shape themselves
into such a small vessel. A name the body alters to fit.

A core of some twenty remained constant, including Amy,
Samuel, Finn, Margaret, Grey, Andrew, Rose, Rosalind
and Duncan, as well as three variations on Catherine.

Her list of sixty-odd names was originally created, in part, for the possibilities of short fiction, during a period when she filled lined yellow foolscap with her sci-fi and fantasy stories.

Moira, whose name rang like a bell. She could not be called anything but what she had been named.

And stop telling people, she said. You make me sound like a crazy person.

2.

Moira. Her mother, attends. A step over threshold.

Their Amelia Catherine was six months old.

During pregnancy, they had discussed the name Zelda. Little Zel. Moira's mother wouldn't hear of it. Besides, the only Zelda anyone knew might have been poor Zelda Fitzgerald. Either that, or the worry that some would assume they'd named their daughter after a video game.

Before Amelia was born, Moira's mother repeated a single name: Annie. Why was she pushing so hard? Mother, they clenched. Given our daughter will most likely be a curly-haired redhead, there is no way in hell we're calling her Annie.

I just like the name, she said, punctuating. Annie.

As they suspected: curly-haired, like her mother. Amelia licks at the banana mush her mother spoons, and swallows.

3.
Dialogue, dialogue. A character crosses the room.

Moira noticed the tendency for friends and strangers alike to gravitate toward the baby and attempt to touch her skin. Moira likened this to disbelief, the improbability that anyone could produce a child. Or did they only think this of her? Everyone in the vicinity concurrently asking, how is this possible? The small, sleeping human you've built. I want to touch her. And in response, Moira recoils, attempts to reabsorb swaddled infant.

The internet provides little salve and few answers. Did this response help you?

Newton's First Law of Motion: a body in motion tends to remain in motion. Let every sleeping baby lie.

Every morning she wakes, and attends to Amelia. Days and nights shapeless, blurred nocturnal stretches of street-lit front room hours in rocking chair. Constantly nursing.

She sinks deep, into the carpet. Moira, who once scored game-winning goals on her high school rugby team, who

saw the swallows return to Capistrano, who held track
and field records in university. She, half-awake in
the dark.

Moira reaches into her chest, wraps hand around heart,
and squeezes.

4.
Amelia, serene in her crib. For Moira, it was the lack
of sleep that surprised her most. Endless, continuous
exhaustion. Nights in the living room sitting with wide-
awake infant. From their east-facing picture window,
she witnessed the sunrise, and newspaper delivery. A car
streaking by like a comet.

As her husband slept, their bedroom door closed. He had
work in the morning.

As her pregnancy grew, Moira read dozens of books on
the subject. Vitamins, exercise, dietary suggestions, and
how her body would stretch. Internal organs pushed
aside. How to pinpoint a flutter of heartbeat.

The tendency to nest: she felt it pull like a magnet.
Blankets wrapped over legs, and her space on the couch
from which she rarely moved. Laptop, stack of baby and
pregnancy titles, and television remote.

5.

Before they knew anything of weddings or babies, the two met for brunch. The first patio weekend of summer in the Byward Market. All sunglasses, and cool. As they settled and sat, an older English gentleman appeared and began reciting the first page of Vladimir Nabokov's *Lolita*. Given she'd read the novel as a teenager, she was familiar enough to recognize it. It felt far too strange for either of them to consider it creepy.

During the same summer, she sent a postcard home to her mother: I am the frozen shores of Lake Ontario.

Through midwife sessions, realizing: she did not know her blood type. It had never occurred to her to find out.

On the train home, she sketched out parts of a crossword that she later abandoned, midway. She had begun to come up against responses that couldn't possibly be right, and wouldn't match up with what else was possible.

6.

The single regret I've had about not birthing children, her aunt once admitted, was the inability to name another human being.

What a responsibility. And what if she were to get it wrong?

Norma Jean had to change her name to Marilyn, so that she could become her. Only then, did crossing that distance seem possible.

Amelia. The name as light as a feather, able to rest on any surface. Amelia, meet pond.

Moira's husband suggested an alternative. We grow into our names, he said. To fill, like a container.

7.

She eases the stroller down sidewalks, slowly memorizing their neighbourhood. Over the five years they'd lived in that house, neither of them had explored the area on foot. She discovers a series of infill houses to the east, and the park at the edge of the greenspace, just down the block. She feels herself open. In turns, Amelia stares, coos, floats back to sleep, occasionally slips out a bowel movement. This too, she learns. Naturally.

During their naps, Moira has begun to dream of domestic matters. She sinks deeper; dreams of making beds, baking bread, laundry cycles, vacuuming, preparing soup in the slow cooker. Her dreams loop: endlessly chopping the same carrots and celery.

8.

Eight months into maternity leave, she feels acclimatized. Moira didn't want to return to work. The job specifics wouldn't have mattered. She did not want to go.

Her days were hard candy: continuous, slow and sweet, but eroding.

What country is it that allows five years of maternity leave? Holland, most likely. Her own mother, provided but three months of leave before she was required to return to work. This seemed inhuman.

Television oddities: reruns of *Secret Agent Man* morphing into *The Prisoner*. Sometimes she feels she is turning invisible. Able to infiltrate any operation, sink through walls, and disappear.

Crumbs and scattered toys. Domestic patter of home-made pastry, stews and baby food. A new language of children's programs, cookbooks and nursery rhymes. Hair clumps stitched to the living room carpet. Was there a name for this, too?

Let me start over, she said to herself. Let me start over.

On beauty

He is always in motion. Two years old, running laps. As part of his opening few weeks of preschool, the teachers, their pickup-time refrain that he is tired, will be tired, must be tired. It was a while before I inquired as to why they were saying this: because he never stopped moving. He would play with everything and everyone in the space without fail, without pause. One thing and one person and then another thing and another person. No, he is not tired, I told them, this is what he is like at home. He never stops moving. I had always assumed this was normal. Was this not normal? Does that make other children more focused, or slower? My wife told me not to worry. I was most likely the same; I am the same now. I can never stop moving. There is still so much that requires attention.

The names of things,

I gave my attention to the pause.
  —*Angela Carr,* Here in There

1.
I am downsizing, for practical reasons. I gift my belongings before the choice is no longer mine. Ending six months of aggressive treatment, some small strength returns. Moving through boxes and bins and shelves, I name items as I release them into the world. I name you, *glass figurines I salvaged from my grandmother's possessions,* as her quiet death ended the decades they sat in her sitting room. I name you, *pilfered coffee mugs,* each adorned with a different company logo.

That summer we drove through the prairies and out to Vancouver, as yet another mug slipped into my bag at a rest stop. You were not amused.

I name you, *dresser*: the scratched and scarred second-hand chassis with lime-green coat over almond brown over deep red over powder blue, plucked from Neighbourhood Services when I was eighteen.

Downsizing, sized. My body erodes. The clothes on my back.

I name you, *silver pocketwatch*: handed down from my
great-grandfather, from his time in Montreal. Now set in
the palm of my sister.

Family lore holds that, during his first decade away from
home, he worked as a conductor for one of the newly
established lines of the Grand Trunk Railway. A decade
saved, and spent, before relocating again with the emer-
gence of a wife and three children, back to his eastern
Ontario nesting grounds, where he gathered a further
fifty-five winters. They say he moved non-stop until he
finally did.

I name you, *small wooden box*, discovered in my mother's
closet. The musty cluster of crumbling paper scraps: correspondence, postcards, a pendant. A locket, held in an
envelope. Dust. Her maiden aunt's engagement ring. This
is all that remains. She, who died when my mother was
young. I name you, *Marjorie*, aunt of my mother.

Heirlooms: objects for which we are but temporary care-
takers, a loom that weaves in and out of the hands of
ancestors, and from mine to my sisters, nieces, nephews.
Brother.

I name you, *long dark curls*, like my mother, back in the
day; as her sisters, too, and their mother as well. Curls
that hadn't the seasons to autumn.

2.

In my youth, I collected; perhaps more than I should
have. I saved, and kept everything. Girl Guide badges,
nuts and bolts from the driveway, miniature carvings of
frogs. I constructed scrapbooks of fauna and flora, a field's
worth of clover. I gathered my late grandfather's wartime diaries, tangible remains secured in a steamer trunk.
I collected a single smooth stone from each childhood
beach, carefully placed on my bedroom bookshelf. From
our suburban infill, a daily memory of a particular Nova
Scotia beach at sunset.

A vial of red sand from Prince Edward Island shores,
St. Margaret's Parish, where my mother's family histori-
cally cottaged. A vial of water from the Athabasca Glacier.
What had once been what it no longer can.

In our first shared apartment, there was the alchemy
of a half-hidden compartment of books in a cupboard,
unlocked. Paperbacks, mostly. Mass-market stuff from
an earlier decade. I immediately decided they were
there precisely for me, and read everything. Susan Dey's
*For Girls Only. The Hawkline Monster. A Brief History
of Time.* I absorbed each one, until there was nothing
unread. Upon our eventual move, more than a couple of
titles managed to slip in among our possessions.

I name you, *library*. I name you, *history*.

3.

I name you, *rage*. I name you, *anger*. A cracked wooden
bowl. Stage four. The one where nothing left can be done.
Meeting with doctors and lawyers and further doctors. I
name you, *comfort*; I name you, *recollection*. I name you,
heartbreak.

In a fever-dream, the moon asks: Why do we melt?

4.

They say to name a thing is to suspend it, freeze it into
a singularity. To name is to reduce, some say. To name
is to provide weight to something otherwise nebulous,
unformed. To name is part of being. Biblical Adam, who
spoke and the animals became what he named; as the
Word of God, also. He speaks, and what has spoken is
solid.

I name instead to remind myself of each object's purpose,
and to provide air.

To make concrete, self-contained, and release.

I have been contemplating both religion and spirituality
lately, but am undecided, as yet.

Soap bubbles, carried away.

5.

I name you, *signed first edition* of Margaret Atwood's *Cat's Eye*, from a lover whose name I've long forgotten. I name you, *soft* and *dear* and *nameless*. I name you, *address book* that belonged to my mother. I name you, *Red Maple leaf*, set between the pages of a hardbound, wax paper saved from summer camp. I name you, *first kiss* by the strawberry bushes. I name you, *lakewater silt* that spawned from our overturned canoe.

I name you, *squeamishness*. Layers of blood, burned brown on white linen.

I name you, *intimacy*. I name you, *pigmentation*. I name you, *jade elephant*.

6.

Lorelei believes that people are a construction of memories and experience, and can be pieced together through what they have abandoned. Nigel remains unconvinced. He claims: We are made up of stories. Without stories, items are stripped of their substance. And yet, once beyond us, they become clean, able to collect anew. Are our possessions allowed lives beyond ours? If no one knows why I owned a jade elephant or where it originated, will that even matter?

I have a jade elephant, attached to a string. Purchased at an outdoor market, I think. London? Paris? I suspect I might be losing my rigorous attention to the integrity of each object.

I consider writing your name on a paper scrap, something I can ingest. Something I might keep.

7.
Terminal illness can't be fixed, it can only be carried. I am putting it down. I release it. From here on, everything lightens. Even my step. Living well, as they say, the finest revenge.

8.
I name you, *school portrait of my first love*, squirreled deep in the pockets of my leather jacket, circa 1995. I name you, *1980s Polaroid of my father at the kitchen window*.

I name you, *shadows*, cast in the doorframe, through hospital blinds.

I name you, *tears of my mother*. I name you, *legs* and *arms*. I name you, *mouth*.

I name you, *morphine*. I name you, *breath*.

Interference

make your mouth noun
shaped now make your hands
  —Pattie McCarthy, Nulls

1.

He vanished long enough ago that he'd most likely been forgotten or declared dead. Possibly both. He'd managed to completely step away from a home, a mortgage and a good paying job. Had anyone noticed? Scattered relatives, perhaps. Most likely long dead, themselves. His sister. He knew his absence would have left few ripples. There might have been rumours. A speck in the news, and then gone.

He'd relocated, changed his name, and quietly settled.

On certain days, he questioned if he even existed, at least in that earlier form. He found comfort in the difference.

2.

1855: the year Dr. David Livingstone became the first European to set eyes upon the waterfalls he would christen after his illustrious queen. The same year British North American backwater Bytown was renamed Ottawa, inching up to a declaration of Capital. The world did not yet exist in photographs.

The colonial mind of Dr. Livingstone, concluding that anything not witnessed by Europeans sat nameless, awaiting. A man of his time.

More than half a century later, from the rubble of the Great War, the British bully who forced a hard line in the sand through the nomadic tribes, and arbitrarily defined the Saudi Arabian border against Iraq. A border held, but never stable.

A mound of bodies is no foundation for a moral high ground.

He writes in his notebook: At times I try to fabricate a memory.

3.
As he spends his days translating dead languages, he wonders: is he reviving, restoring or speeding up their demise? Words that haven't been spoken aloud for decades. The sounds and shapes of the disappeared.

4.
There was an article making the rounds on social media: the discovery of ten previously unknown works attributed to the late Group of Seven painter

J.E.H. MacDonald. The paintings had sat forty years wrapped in plastic and buried, before unearthed to see another four decades locked up in storage.

The discovery was remarkable, albeit confusing. Who buries paintings for safekeeping?

London during the Blitz, or wartime Berlin. But who buries paintings in Ontario?

5.
He took a healthy bite of his Golden Delicious, and his gums began to bleed.

6.
He told himself there was a diner he liked to frequent, but if he were to map out his movements, he would realize he hadn't actually set foot inside for more than a dozen years. Whenever in or near the neighbourhood, he would recall the diner with fondness, his memories held in amber, replaying the same limited scenes.

The city had become less a lived experience than a sequence of recollections.

It took him two years to realize the building had been replaced with condos, luxury living constructed over his beloved, ignored space.

7.

She texts her mother: I now understand the beauty of the missing piece.

I am dying, Egypt.

8.

The community of Fort McMurray, Alberta, is ravaged by a devastating fire. All cinders and ash, more than one hundred thousand hectares. He can't even fathom.

In the 1870s, his great-grandfather had an uncle who disappeared en route to the Klondike: the lure of gold and the myth of the self-created man. His ancestor could have died or settled anywhere in-between, or landed to discover his fortune, change his name and eventually marry, seeding the west with descendants. They might never know.

Fort McMurray: he nearly ended up there, himself. Decades of culture reducing the municipality of Wood Buffalo to an oil-rich feed, a black northern hole in which to disappear and re-emerge, cash in hand. There were times he'd been tempted. Now: reports on the news about how offensive the subject of climate change is for the relocated populace. How dare you mention. Others blame premier, prime minister. Sad opportunists.

He wonders: with the people, the occupants, gone, even temporarily, who will strip the oil from the earth?

9.

Had J.D. Salinger not enlisted, perhaps his girlfriend, Oona O'Neill, daughter of Eugene O'Neill, might never have left him. Perhaps she might not have abandoned New York for Los Angeles. Perhaps she might never have married Charlie Chaplin, thirty-six years her senior, who would father her small mound of children. Eight, in all.

Some might escape, but their troubles follow. You can't leave behind what is buried within.

She sends a message to her sister. Fucker broke up with me over email. Twenty-two years.

10.

There was the teenage girl who ran away from home, only to move three houses down in her tiny Ontario hamlet. Where her family had been for generations. She dyed her hair and expected no one to notice.

11.

The difficulty with which one is able to disappear. Proper planning is essential. Decades ago it was different: there were the adventure-seekers who travelled west for the gold rush, or those who floated across the American border and lied about their age and country, to join military ranks. The ease with which one might shift. The legends of D.B. Cooper. Back when a girl could leave school for a season and return, following the inevitable announcement of newborn sibling. Some might suspect, but most would never know.

Their bodies and lives, shaped to their stories. Whether lies, reinventions or salvation.

Some way out of here. I must find.

Seven impossible things

I did not know
when I began I'd fill these poems
with so much information
    —*Heather Christle,* Heliopause

1.

Any time I open a new novel, I start by reading the
final line on the final page. Only then can I start at the
beginning.

2.

She rolls her eyes. She tells me that this has much to do
with my fear of the unknown. You need to know how
it ends, she says, otherwise you refuse to engage with
the process. You have to know everything that happens
before it actually does.

But reading the final sentence doesn't reveal anything
about how the book might end. It only tells you the
ending. It says nothing about what that might mean.

3.

Fear. She claims I'm ruled by it. You barely leave the house in the morning until you know what we're having for dinner. You refuse to be spontaneous.

4.

What exactly is fear? Fear is about being unprepared.

I never craved the ending. I want to understand the ending, and how it occurs. I want to understand how we arrive.

5.

What Obi-Wan Kenobi said in *Star Wars*, suggesting his years of post-traumatic stress disorder: "I felt a great disturbance in the Force, as if millions of voices suddenly cried out in terror and were suddenly silenced. I fear something terrible has happened."

It was only the passage of time that allowed his return.

6.

Thousands of times over are people killed by guns than, say, Ebola. Ebola was quickly registered as a crisis. We can't talk about guns.

7.

Lately I've been thinking about the Greeks. They had a system for everything. How the ancient Greeks annually banished a resident selected through community vote.

Whoever was selected would be banished for a period of ten years, after which they were, if they wished, welcome to return.

Ten years. He could be dead by then.

8.
They say light travels at a particular speed. The speed of light.

A fixed point. How the temperature of any room is not necessarily "room temperature."

There is the optical trick of seeing the same light-object in multiple points in space simultaneously. There is the knowledge that all we see in the heavens are stars and galaxies tens of thousands of years dead and disappeared by the time we even notice.

9.
I am talking about how the sun always sets. How the sun also rises.

This is something we take for granted. How did we get here?

10.
After all this time, my mother still dead. How is this possible.

The city is uneven

Always in Alberta there is a fresh wind blowing.
  —*Nellie McClung,* The Stream Runs Fast

1.
Soon this space will be too small.

This is what I am trying to tell you: I am attempting to
make it out of the middle.

The middle of what?

2.
This conversation occurs in a repurposed church, as part of
a literary festival. Her third such festival in the space of
weeks. Perhaps this particular exchange occurs only in her
head.

They were here to discuss Alberta's first book in more
than a decade. They declared: a triumph, a departure,
a return.

Anglican-grey stone walls and tempered wood. Given the
setting, she is conscious to refrain from cursing, and makes
a joke of it during her reading. She recalled Christmas
services from childhood, and the blessings of the water.
Her mother's belief in what the blessings provide.

Alberta wonders: if this is a return, where had she been?
The same desk in the same small room, scratching away.
The penance of Sisyphus.

She squirms in her seat, attempting to not sound ridicu-
lous. As part of the onstage interview, she is asked about
the intervening time since the publication of her previous
novel. What were you doing?

The audience falls on a hush.

Alberta, startled. Writing, she says. I was writing.

They act as though she returns from the dead.

3.
Her home office, with south-facing window directly
across from their neighbour's stained-glass. Months
of David Bowie's *Heroes* on repeat, lining the walls and
coating the bookshelves.

One sentence, compounding.

Her house constructed on former farmland. Prehistoric
grasses force their way through the patio interlock, and
puncture the garden. The occasional outcrop of rabbit,
or stone.

Their bungalow roughly seventy-five years old, constructed in what was once the outskirts of the capital. Now they may as well live in the centre. One street over, the houses are thirty years old, but most that surround hers are of similar vintage, if not slightly older.

The ghosts of dead livestock. A cornfield across the adjoining lot.

Despite the years, she occasionally forgets: a house purchased as a pair, now singularly owned.

4.
Mx. Her daughter claims the genderless prefix. She concurrently understands, and is baffled. She wishes to remain supportive, but finds the question confusing. How has her daughter changed? Or has the change always been?

One question leads to another, which only seems to antagonize. Alberta, who asks about plumbing, and is met with hostility. Once again, she's informed, you've completely missed the point.

When change is constant, it becomes fixed. Perhaps, she realizes, this is who her daughter was all along.

5.
Emerged. Alberta refuses the word. It implies she had lapsed into some kind of pit, and perhaps she had. Spring forth, novel.

Fully formed, of course. At least that's what the newspaper profile suggests. A decade of resting on her laurels and sitting on her hands, as her novel sighed out of her.

Too old for this ongoing, restless rage. Everything her novel attempted to purge.

The book was published, and yet, remained in her belly. Until this tour ended, it would not disengage: they shared a bloodstream. She could not find her distance.

Granted, it took longer than it should have. She wrote and wrote and revised, abandoning far more than she'd written, running waist-deep through plots, purpose and pondering. So much time reworking and so little accomplished.

Graham, on his deathbed. Recalling her *Mrs. Dalloway*: sometimes it takes a death to prompt the rest into living.

But he'd been dying for so long.

She might not be free until the first sentence of her next book.

6.

The latest review concludes: "This is a book of transitions, composed between point of origin and destination, neither of which are described or explained but through absence...writing out what can only be determined through experience."

7.

Eden posits, re-posits. Pronouns. Hones a personal precision. A clarification. How does one explain to one such as their mother? The prefix so much less important than the stem, but the wrong one throws off all meaning. Eden's mother focused entirely on the wrong things. As per usual.

There is so much that shouldn't need to be said.

This is Eden's articling year: a fidelity beyond the billable hour. A recycled math that evaporates, but for the admission of so many more hours that will remain unpaid. The archivist, paid to research; the lawyer, not. Is all of this research?

From co-workers: how shall we address you? Emily, shifting to Eden. An interior monologue that requires stifling, while crafting bad jokes, including "Sir Mx-a-Lot," or "Hits and Mrs." Such terrible puns. The kind that would cause Eden's mother to rankle, to consider beneath them. How could she contain such a love of language but a lack of appreciation for the pun? As Eden, in darker moments, has described the language of Alberta's novels: all work, and no play.

Get me to the point on time.

8.

What did Alberta expect of writing? What does
she, still? Over the years, her answer has changed.
Accomplishment, attention, occasional accolade. Back
to the beginning.

Alive only as long as one remains in print.

The ancient Chinese, who recorded no history because
they saw the world as cyclical. Here, again. I am. *The
Odyssey* and *The Wizard of Oz*: both books about home,
and the pull to return. Adventures, be damned.

If all roads lead to Rome, so too, all roads lead away.
Telescopic.

9.

"She was loath to admit," Alberta writes, "but she dreaded
the lake."

On beauty

Upon the death of her widower father, there came the matter of dismantling his possessions. Emptying and cleaning the house for resale. It wasn't as though either of the children were planning on returning to the homestead, both some twenty years removed, but it fell to them to pick apart the entirety of their parents' lives from out of this multi-level wooden frame, a structure originally erected by their grandfather and great-grandfather immediately following the Great War. Theirs was the first house in the area, constructed on seventy-five acres of farmland, long since disappeared to development. Across the street, a smaller house of similar design and build, where the hired man and his family had lived. Where, originally, their widowed great-grandmother spent her final days, sixteen long years past the death of her husband.

The house was a local oddity, an obvious construction decades before the brown brick and stone-grey on either side, and contemporary infills. Where the neighbouring bungalow was once their back garden; another, where livestock spent fallow days. Where most likely a barn stood, then a shed, which now hold driveway and garage. Foundation maintenance that routinely uncovers the roots of an orchard. The difficulty of inground pools, and the puncture of linings.

Their father's house: now that he was dead, it was though it had died as well. They had no choice but to bury it. Not a word. Silence. My wife and her sister, dismantling what would never exist again, and by dismantling, removing it from all but their memory. This, too, will fade.

The telltale heart,

Make an illogical jump—dissociation—but, then, imper-
ceptibly—so, quickly—return to render it logical before
anyone has seen. In this way, you may seem to improve
upon reason.
    —*Lucy Ives,* The Hermit

Character #1:
When I told you she was grieving her mother, I wasn't
trying to imbue her with impossible loss but to provide
evidence of how deeply she loves.

Character #2:
When I named him Arturus—an older, antiquated name—
I wanted to suggest a sublime, absurd weight. I was
curious to see if he could find his way out from under it.

Character #3:
Every morning he woke to the same thought: I should
walk down to see if there's something I need at the thrift
store. It wasn't boredom, obsession or greed, but how he'd
adapted to loneliness.

Character #4:
When I told you that, as a boy, he'd lived a week undiscov-
ered in a department store, I was adapting a news item

I'd heard on the radio. I was attracted to the magical elements, akin to British traditions of children's fiction. Implausible does not mean impossible; most of the time, not even "impossible" is impossible.

Character #5:
When I introduced a fact that seemingly contradicted the rest, it was that very conflict I sought. We are human, and thus, often make no damned sense.

Character #6:
Most of the details I offer are constructed, woven from numerous threads of maybes and what-ifs. Being "true" doesn't mean it occurred. Any experienced reader of fiction should already know this.

Characters #7 and #8:
When I described the theft of her bicycle and, further on, the bicycle thief, one might suspect I'd be suggesting a link. As of yet, any connection between the two remains unverified.

Character #9:
When I described Emily's preference for Bombay Sapphire, I was, in fact, suggesting an unconscious response to her mother's years of half-hidden drink, and her latent fear of becoming her. It was never about her father. It was, as they say, a red herring.

Character #10:

When I finally baptized him Malcolm, it was toward
the end of an unrelated conversation about collabora-
tive naming during our second and final pregnancy. Our
list of male names also included Grey, Samuel (which
I'd rejected), Finley ("Finn") and Erich. Once we were
informed that our final child was female, our list of
male names was immediately set aside. Only then did
she admit she was warming to Malcolm as baby name.
Through finally naming a long-nameless character,
I was attempting to reclaim that potential.

Character #11:

When I described her parents as older, it was to allow for
a distance between generations. I wanted to give her a bit
more independence, and possibly expand her patience.
I removed her father quickly, as I wanted to explore
the currents and complications between mothers and
daughters.

I made her a swimmer because I enjoyed the irony
of a girl from the prairies obsessed with swimming.
She needed something that belonged entirely to her,
especially something that, on the surface, appeared non-
sensical. Perhaps it merely showcased my own prairie
ignorance. When she later abandoned swimming, it
allowed for the bittersweet memory. Once she was
mature enough to reconsider and recover elements of her
childhood, it could both soothe and distract.

I named her Alberta because it is such a striking name
for a girl. Because I wanted her to hold your attention.
And to imply the well-intentioned optimism of her parents, naming their daughter for a destination they never
achieved.

Character #12:
When I spoke of her, it was through the lens of my mother's illness, and not Alzheimer's, as some have suggested.
I find that particular reading curious. To date, this is the
closest I've written my mother.

And yet, when I write "I," I am not necessarily writing as
"writer" but as "narrator," which is, also, a fiction.

Character #13:
When the story opens, I did not mention their gender
because it wasn't relevant. That is, until it was.

Character #14:
I've always been interested in how individuals shape
themselves to a variety of external elements, such as their
name, as liquid to its container. When I articulated the
prominence of what she was named, it was to display the
difference in what she preferred to be called. This was not
to highlight her shift beyond how they had known her,
but her own comfort upon becoming. She was, and simply
required those around her to acknowledge.

Character #11:

When I returned to the same character at a point years after I'd last written her, it was to take stock of someone I felt I'd described so completely in her time and her place that I wanted to see where she would end up. I wanted to see what had become of her, and where she had gone. I wanted to know what her choices had led her to. I wanted to know if she was happy.

Character #15:

When I attempt to articulate how certain characters move from point A to point B, I am less interested in the details of points-of-origin or destination than the journey itself. I am interested, instead, in the result of actions, which then lead to further action. How did they get here?

Character #16:

When I spoke of my father, it was a fiction based on carefully selected facts. I lied about everything else.

Green, with a pleasant breeze

cold is made of beauty and fear
and thaw is made of aching.
    —*Sarah Gordon,* Rapture Red & Smoke Grey

1.

Not long after they married, Malcolm glimpsed an article
via his Facebook feed that included a list of realities associated with a long-term marriage. "There will be times
when you feel unfulfilled," it read. "There will be times
when you hate your spouse." The list was not created to
frighten, but to allow for a more successful union; to pre-
vent couples from falling prey to the myth of constant
magic.

The honeymoon, as poet Michael Redhill once wrote: the
time that life pays you for in advance.

Malcolm considered the article a relief. More than he
might have guessed. It became important later, as they
had a brief period, a moment, that might easily have
broken them. They wished to remain together. They
remained together.

2.

Had you known him when he was ten years old, you might understand the hours he spent in his room listening to a numbers station via shortwave radio. He'd already filled dozens of spiral-bound notebooks with as many as he could capture: 1 2 23 2 7 54 76 76 98 6 43 4 8 54 78 10 9 4 89 5 3.

He found the feminine speaking voice soothing. Hypnotic. The hours would vanish.

He was attempting to discern a pattern. He was convinced it was important, and something only he could decipher. He just had to write down enough for the shape to reveal itself.

Malcolm's entire study was predicated on a single premise: the non-existence of randomness. Convinced that, once he had collected enough information, he could discern a pattern; and once a pattern, a system. A thoroughness was required. Patience.

3.

More recently, after a shared family dinner, Malcolm and Liam settled into the backyard, beer bottles in hand. Malcolm cradled his sleeping newborn in a green Celtic-designed ring-sling. Inside, their spouses attempted to settle their three combined toddlers.

Liam shuffled, seemed more awkward than usual. He does admit to a disconnect with his wife. Malcolm has noticed Liam's wandering attention. His brother says: It's like I don't know her anymore. Since the twins. There is always someone else in the way.

We can easily watch the boys if you need a night out, Malcolm offers. Liam turned his face to the yard in that way that their father had. In that way that ended conversation.

There was silence enough to solidify.

Malcolm sighed. You should talk to your wife.

4.

At eighteen, Malcolm worked a summer as a short-term receptionist in a government office. It meant shapeless hours of solitude, recirculated air, and artificial light, peppered with pockets of meaningless small talk. It meant that he spent his days shifting paper from files and piles, and answering calls for three or four different managers throughout the department. Whenever he was struck by a particularly foul mood, he would forward calls to his unsuspecting, and often sleeping, roommate. Hysterical. His roommate never did figure out where those calls were from. And Malcolm knew, had the office not been too cheap to upgrade their antiquated phone system, he couldn't have gotten away with it.

5.

Malcolm deliberately avoids comparing Moira to his first wife. The past truly is a foreign country.

Czeslaw Milosz wrote: The past is *inaccurate.*

6.

Malcolm rails at the television. Yet another sitcom plot founded on a romantic couple's lack of communication. One lies to the other, and the predictable mayhem ensues with hilarious consequences. Between such examples of why couples should be more honest and open, and the American sitcom's conservative views on sex, do sitcom writers really consider themselves to be protectors of the moral realms? A laugh prompt: so we know when something is supposed to be funny.

Are people as dim-witted as anyone on television? And why would he think that they should be?

7.

When he was seven years old, his father died of a brain aneurysm. Barely into his forties. He fell to the ground and was gone. He kept falling. He is falling still.

At forty-two, Malcolm has outlived his father by six months, making him the oldest of any of the men in his family in three generations. The realization unsettled him.

Sorting through his father's belongings for donation, Malcolm had salvaged a white T-shirt with logo and slogan that read "All American." He pulled it from the assortment and made it his own. For months, Malcolm wore it with an awkward pride. He didn't know what it meant. He was seven years old; he didn't really know what anything meant.

8.

An internet meme suggests listing the lessons you'd want to impart to your younger self. Malcolm usually ignored such online distraction, but he couldn't shake the idea. He was less concerned with what he might say than just how and where to actually find his childhood self. Would he slip into a corner of the schoolyard, there by the fence-line, hoping to discover his school-age self alone? Would he return to the homestead, staking out the front or back-yard, or attempt to slip into the house, unseen? Would he scale the TV antenna tower and rap on his bedroom window? He would be an adult, technically stalking a child.

He remembers how foolish he was. How shy, naïve and sullen. To witness that might just be unbearable.

On beauty

During our first pregnancy, she suggested we each write letters to eventually gift to our as-yet-unborn child. She described it as a kind of journal-keeping, rehearsing self-portraits through our accumulated hopes. It was a solid idea, but one difficult to maintain. I spent two months sketching out paragraphs, regularly dipping into the file on my laptop, but then ran out of steam. During our second pregnancy, neither of us wanted to even bring up the idea, embarrassed by how little we'd accomplished the first time around.

The last words spoken on the surface of the moon

You do not know what the other bodies imagine.
   —Margaret Christakos, Her Paraphernalia

1.

Before they could move into the new house, the city managed to obliterate it. A mistake, they were told. A matter of blocks from a house scheduled for demolition, and instead, a single hydraulic behemoth erased what was to be their first home. Two numbers switched in the four-digit address and the work crew landed at the wrong door. It took less than an hour. She's described it since as a sandcastle, set against tide.

Given they'd ended their lease, it now meant stowing crates and furniture into long-term storage. Runoff set in his father's garage, his mother's sewing room.

She mourned. *They took our house.* The moonscape of interrupted earth on their lot. With a brand-new mortgage, they were suddenly homeless. A filled-in crater that had harboured their deepest hopes.

2.

In her small studio, she spent part of the morning
sketching a torso. Black marks across ribcage, ribcage,
tenor. It quickly devolved into a blacktop of rage.

3.

It was her third pregnancy, and the first to achieve a
second trimester. Nearing the end of the sixth month,
everything a haze. Her blood pressure rose soft at first,
and then further. She lived in a haze. Did I already say
that? There was little else: her energy, eroded. Spilled out.

At least, she had no double vision. Not yet. Her doctors
their eye upon. Midwives, as well. Her last chance at
babies, and now, she was a desert; with boundless emo-
tions, she'd already cried herself dry.

Reclining on her mother-in-law's couch, she attempted
deep breaths. She changed, with the tides. There was a tug
on her, some. Just there. And she, in no position to resist.

She was as soft as water, as dry as a dune.

4.

Her mother's ashes. She had set the metal urn on the
hardwood, in the centre of what once was their living
room. What would have been.

Her mother, erased down to nothing, all over again.
Where she lay in the lot.

5.

When they first saw the house, it was their fourth that
day, and fifteenth overall. Their realtor, Donna, hopping
from driveway to driveway across multiple neighbour-
hoods. A cat and mouse of two cars.

When they pulled into the rumpled driveway, this house
felt different. A hedge, carport. Stained glass above side
door. The smell of the rosebushes. A humming, nearly a
sing-song.

When Donna's back was turned, when his was turned too,
everything spoke.

Marry me, said the yard. Said the sandbox. Two squirrels.

I do not wish to marry any of you, she replied. I do not
wish to marry anyone. But I will live here.

6.

He did a lot of yelling into the phone. He involved lawyers, police. Normally, she would have dealt with
whatever came next, but she could barely see straight.
He did so much yelling during that time, although never
at her. And only in regard to their house, their beautiful
dream-house.

She lay an afternoon on the couch in her grandmother's family room. This was the room with the furniture

covered in plastic, and ceramic telephone with gold trim. Where the piano was held, in front of the wall hanging. An embroidered stag, in the wood. Where children were forbidden—seen, and not heard.

Until she was pregnant, her grandmother had refused her entry. Not in here, she said. Now her grandmother gave her wide margin, and the occasional cup of tea. Drink this, she would tell her, spooning in honey.

7.

Lawyers, guns and money. She'd been listening nonstop to Warren Zevon, awash in some kind of adolescent retreat. I won't come out, she told him. She told them; she told anyone.

Space Camp, he named her. She had been thrice as a teen, heading down into Florida for extended periods of exploration. Most of her peers from each group had gone on to work at NASA.

Once she'd announced this new pregnancy, the first she'd been able to, the television series she'd been appearing in had shifted her occasional role. "She enters the room carrying a laundry basket." "She remains behind a counter the entire scene." By the time she'd progressed, they'd finally found some reason to write her out of the show entirely.

Erase, erase. She was *mother* now, and then nothing. At least, nothing else.

8.

Gel on her belly, tingly-cool. This is their third appointment with the same ultrasound technician for the sake of measuring the baby's heart. Their baby, head down and spine out, uncooperative. The third scan in which the technician admits she still can't determine a gender. At least, not decisively. She could guess, but that wouldn't be useful. Fine, they say, fine. This is alright. They can wait.

On the monitor, she sees her baby's heartbeat, the creepy outline of her baby's small skull, unintentional grin, and she weeps. Silent, and happily bursting. She cries each time they go in. Her healthy, recalcitrant baby.

Their list of baby names expands and contracts, exponentially, until it finally peaks, and begins to reduce down to reason. They are so close.

9.

After six weeks, new construction finally began on the lot. A clean slate.

She imagines her mother's spirit blended into every inch of the property, every piece of the house. And she is pleased.

The Man from Glengarry

I am the foreigner. I am the prodigal who hates the foreigner.
—*Michael Ondaatje,* Running in the Family

1.
He asks himself: To be from somewhere, does that mean you are also of that same place? And what is the difference? Perhaps these are the incorrect questions.

There are those of the county that consider it a Celtic creation, but tend not to give any thought to the Mohawk, displaced from the land before the establishment of European boundaries. Dismissed by the British with no more than a word that erases their agency: *acquired*. Do you even know where they went, where they ended up? Without explanation, or further context. Instead, we speak of brawny Scottish pioneers who tamed the trees and rapids and the roughness of bush, intemperate and desolate and snow-thick. The swamps they'd cross to drain, and drain to cross.

The land is sacred, their descendants trill, without a speck of irony. I mean, what matters?

2.

During every teenhood summer, the drinking deaths
involving speeding cars that met with trains or met
with trees or met with other cars. The year one car
flipped, four bodies linking arms from across the provincial border, returning home from a village bar out of
sight but not out of reach. A year to the day later, a train
struck another, as metal and adolescence lay dead on the
tracks. By 11 p.m., most of the farm kids long in bed, buff-
ered from such summer danger: bored teens driving
roughshod, cross-stitch over blacktop, watching mail-
boxes, driveways, fields of sleepy Holsteins, trees and
trees and forests for the trees and desperately searching
for how to leave this place but unable to cross that final
boundary. Car radios or cassette decks blasting PJ Harvey
or blasting Depeche Mode or blasting whatever else into
that combustion of county silence and oblivion, driving
out or into what they could not see to escape, what they
could not hope to contain.

They say it is raining on Lake Michigan. In which direction is that?

3.

1881: an upside-down year. The year William Henry
McCarty Jr., also known as William H. Bonney, "Billy
the Kid," was shot and killed by Pat Garrett outside Fort
Sumner, New Mexico. The year the fictional Dr. John H.
Watson was introduced to Sherlock Holmes, opening

A Study in Scarlet. The year the Canadian Pacific Railway
was incorporated, and Lakota Sioux Chief Sitting Bull
surrendered to US federal troops. Over the space of this
same year, US President James A. Garfield was inaugu-
rated, shot and soon died, replaced by Chester A. Arthur.
The census found 4,324,810 people living in Canada, and
the borders of Manitoba stretched farther north, west
and east, causing Ontario, of course, to complain.

This was also the year the rail line scratched to meet the
earth of the county, delineating a single east–west line,
around which a hamlet begin to eddy, swirl. A station that
begat a hamlet, then a village, draining out surrounding
hamlets, some down to but a single homestead. A pool
that grew enough to village but no more, they say, for
the lack of an accompanying body of water. Still. From
the gravity well of trestle, the promise of passenger and
freight, a billow-belch of Victorian smoke enough to parallel the treeline, sky.

A lineage, a path, along a delta of farmland, the layered
blues of Prescott and Russell along the northern boundary.
And here, just south, from this line down through two
centuries of familial activity, stretch of trees and seasonal
pine and pick of stone to line the fence, the underbrush.

4.
From the isolation, and a blend of Scottish, Irish and
French, an Ottawa Valley lilt, or twang: the kind that adds

an *h*, shifting *room* to the phonetic *rhoom*, amusing any
number of listeners from beyond the borders of Ottawa
Valley. Our history-rich parcel of eastern Ontario: the
transition between the St. Lawrence Lowlands and the
Canadian Shield, still known as unceded territory, tradi-
tionally that of the Algonquin First Nations.

Amid rolling logs and sawdust trails, the sound of chain-
saws. Domtar cleans away the deadwood, a managed
forest signed along the mess of muddy ditch, of spring.

They say it is raining on the Ottawa River. The storm
rides the river, galloping west. We see no evidence from
here.

5.

My father's annual cow that bleeds out in the shed, front-
end loader, chained-up legs of carcass over concrete floor,
as gravity leans a line into a dark red pool. A cat carcass
asleep in the haymow, pitchfork assailing it out through
the window and down into muddy barnyard.

At the top of the laneway, aside the mailbox, he waits for
his morning school bus amid the red-winged blackbirds.
Birdsong permeates the clear spring air, the combined
sweet scent of mud, dead grass and melting snow.

They say it is raining on the St. Lawrence River, where
boats would roam for pleasure. The occasional nighttime

run for cigarettes. Along the coastline, bullet holes adorn the outer walls. They, greyscale, shadow. Much like this rain.

6.

A tether, neither anchor nor umbilical. What else to call it. Look, he says, to his trio of daughters. This geography as much a part of my body as you. He waves his hand. They roll their eyes.

The secret origins of the everyday

Once upon a time there was a little boy and a little girl
who lived in different places
and didn't know each other.
   —*Ken Sparling,* This Poem Is a House

1.

There is such an obvious shift in scent and air pressure before it rains. I don't understand how my wife remains immune to it.

It is going to rain, I tell her. Sunday morning, we stand adjacent to swings assisting preschooler, swinging. She might not agree with my assessment, but we make our way home from the playground, avoiding the downpour by minutes.

There is a word for this.

2.

A fragment of Ray Bradbury's *The Martian Chronicles* still unsettles: the house that outlived its occupants, their shadows burned into exterior wall. As a pre-teen, I saw the back of our farmhouse as the house in the story and still do.

The family dog, collapsed dead on the porch.

There are things that we carry, that we are unable to set down again. Fictions, both real and imagined.

As Dany Laferrière wrote: I am writing this book to save my life. I am nestled in bracken and thorny brambles, scribbling my freedom in margins.

I am Peter Rabbit, deep in the undergrowth. The fox can never find me.

3.
I take off my coat. She takes off her coat.

The toddler kicks off boots, tosses coat to the floor.

One for sorrow, two for mirth.

4.
Certain British literature for children espouses bored offspring in school uniforms, whether singularly or along-side siblings, cousins or friends, dispatched to neither be seen nor heard, and who unearth something magical. Our attics connect, and we rummage around until we find something ancient, abandoned and possibly cursed. An egg nestled in the flying carpet we salvaged from thrift. The interior of the wardrobe is endless, and expands into snowy exterior.

And yet, no child questions: Why are we only discovering this now? What else have they kept from us? Curiosity, pushing fearlessly past storage of winter coats.

The Canadian show *Read All About It!* and its abandoned coach house that held printing presses, and the steamer trunk that allowed the kids to travel through time. Hello, 1812. Hello, Laura Secord and Major-General Sir Isaac Brock.

Our century-old farmhouse was always a disappointment. There were no hidden doors or corridors, and the back of my parents' walk-in sheltered no secret compartments. Our house held no ghosts.

Perhaps the lesson here is one of discernment, and more subtle, archaeological clues. We dug around for the obvious, unable to understand yet how real secrets are kept.

5.
She calls through the baby monitor, crying. I had a bad dream.

I touch down on toddler bed, to comfort her. She says: I don't like thoughts. What are they? I had a bad thought about a shark and a mermaid.

Dreams are stories our heads make up. The more I repeat this, the more I begin to believe it.

Winnie-the-Pooh: I'm just a little black rain cloud.

6.

The shelter of privilege. Had I been born in another time, I might already be dead. My babies might already be dead. Had I been born in another place, I might already be dead or imprisoned, my lands stolen from under me. My wife and our babies. Had I been born with a different pigmentation, I might already be dead. My babies, targeted. My wife, dead. At what point does comprehension unsettle enough to become action, including my own?

7.

After three years, I haven't quite managed the basics of gardening. I plant, water and weed, and then, somehow, don't bother again for days. The sun bakes and the weeds, overtake.

Our neighbour from across the street rings our doorbell and gifts us a small bag of tomatoes. After introducing himself, he says that they had overrun his backyard. More than he knows what to do with, he says.

A week later, I return the gesture, gifting a fresh loaf of banana bread. There is no such thing as too much.

8.

Stephen Reid posts a photo to Facebook, with caption:
This is where we hid out in the bad old days as the
Stopwatch Gang.

Sedona, Arizona: a desert town by Flagstaff, surrounded
by red-rock buttes, steep canyon walls and pine forests. This is where decades of bandits lay hidden, fresh
from robbing banks and trains and covered wagons. A
Canadian trio of bank robbers, they were ever in tune
with history.

The Stopwatch Gang: the opposite of gunslingers.

9.

Returning home from mid-week work, my wife calls out a
greeting. She places car keys upon the kitchen island, and
hangs up her coat. How was your day?

The first snow coats everything: our unkempt lawn, and
the scattering of backyard chairs and toys I have yet to
gather.

Toddler drifts through the ends of her nap. Dinner warms
in the oven.

Half-asleep in the living room, I've put all my faith into
Brian Eno recordings. Today's entry: Bang on a Can,
Music for Airports.

Her voice down the runway.

10.
A recent fan theory posits that the character Sandy in the musical *Grease* had drowned, and the entire movie was her coma-dream.

Half-joking, my wife counters: Must you take everything from me?

11.
We return from the orchard, two Empire bags richer. My dear wife's suggestion that, at least every week or two, we participate in some kind of family outing. Today it was off to an orchard in the east end, with a side trip for groceries in a suburban big-box store. In another few weeks, a morning around the collection of a singular pumpkin, due south. The toddler is thrilled.

Post-orchard, apple bags are relegated to the sunroom. Over subsequent days, I prepare apple bread, applesauce, pies. I contemplate jam, even as toddler gnaws at a core. Scrape the burnt sauce from the floor of the pot for a week.

12.
There are days in which I can't discern how anything connects.

This is but one.

On beauty

Wake by 6 a.m. Put the kettle on for toddler's oatmeal, start coffee. Slip into the washroom, splash my face with water. Quickly dress. Kettle boils. Slide a bowl of oatmeal in front of eager toddler, check email, collect my newspaper from the front step. Coffee. A second bowl of oatmeal. Wife prepares herself for work, checks her phone, dresses, puts on makeup, interacts with now-fed toddler. I read my newspaper. My wife heads to work. Gather toddler, diaper change and clean clothes from the bin, offer his snow pants to begin the process of heading out. He dresses, slowly, allowing another sip of coffee. I make a quick stop in the washroom, and brush teeth. Collect keys, adjust his coat and boots. Collect his backpack and own coat, boots, before out the door by 8:45. This will be a good day. This will be a good day.

Acknowledgements

"The Matrix Resolutions" appeared online in *The Puritan* (Toronto, ON). "Art I have not made" appeared in *Matrix* (Montreal, QC). "A short film about my father" appeared online in Douglas Glover's *Numéro Cinq* (NY). "Fourteen things you don't know about Arturus Booth" appeared in *Grain Magazine* (Saskatoon, SK). "Character sketch" appeared online in *Atlas Review* (Brooklyn, NY). "Silence" appeared online in *Control Literary Magazine* (US). "Opening" appeared in print and online in *The New Quarterly* (Waterloo, ON). "The New House" appeared online in *matchbook* (Buffalo, NY). "Less than zero: five imaginary stories," and "The telltale heart," appeared online in *Entropy* (US). "Baby names" appeared online in *The Danforth Review* (Toronto, ON). "Swimming lessons" appeared online in *Hippo Reads* (Santa Monica, CA). "The city is uneven" appeared in *PRISM international* (Vancouver, BC). "Fearless" appeared in the "Borders" issue of *The Windsor Review* (Windsor, ON), and subsequently in *Release Any Words Stuck Inside of You: An* untethered *Collection of Shorts* (Toronto, ON: Applebeard Editions, 2018). "Seven impossible things" appeared online at *Synapse* (Montreal, QC). "The secret origins of the everyday" appeared online at *Bad Nudes* (Montreal, QC). "The last words spoken on the surface of the moon" appeared online at *JMWW* (US). "A dream about vegetable soup" appeared online at *The Airgonaut* (US). "Interference" appeared online at *Fixtional* (NC). "Songs my mother taught me," appeared online at *Queen Mob's Teahouse* (UK). "Things to do in airports" appeared online at *Pithead Chapel* (MI). "Interruptions" appeared in *ELQ/Exile* (Holstein, ON), and later on the author's clever Substack. "The names of things," appeared online in *X-R-A-Y Literary Magazine* (Phoenix, AZ). "Bicycle" appeared online at *Bending Genres* (NM), and later via the author's Substack. "The Garden" appeared online in the first issue of *Fat Cat* (US).

"Character sketch," "A short film about my father," "Silence" and "The city is uneven" also appeared as the chapbook *Four Stories* (Ottawa, ON: Apostrophe Press, 2016), produced as a handout for an event at the University of Alberta, March 2016, celebrating the fortieth anniversary of their Writer-in-Residence Program. A larger selection of stories appeared in the chapbook *Imaginary Stories* (Ottawa, ON: DevilHousePress, 2017). "The city is uneven" was also a finalist for *The Best Small Fictions 2017* (Braddock, PA: Braddock Avenue Books).

My thanks to all the editors and publishers involved. The individual sections of this volume's title story appeared intermittently on the author's own blog during the fall and winter of 2016–17.

The title "Green, with a pleasant breeze" is borrowed from Lydia Millet's untitled fiction from the anthology

Significant Objects: 100 Extraordinary Stories About Ordinary Things (Seattle, WA: Fantagraphics Books, 2012).

The quotation from Philip Roth in this volume's epigraph appeared in "You'll Never Write About Me Again" by Livia Manera Sambuy (*The Believer*, January/February 2015, Issue #111).

Much thanks to Sara Cassidy for feedback on "Swimming lessons" and "Christmas music," and to Brenda Liefso for feedback on "Swimming lessons." Much thanks to Natalee Caple, Michelle Berry and Rod Moody-Corbett for essential feedback and conversation once the manuscript began to find shape. Thanks also to middle daughter Rose for feedback on "The Last Man on Earth" and "A short film about my father" during the final stages of editing. With special thanks to Christine McNair for her support and patience (as well as her own feedback on more than a couple of stories), and Karin McNair for occasional childcare, without whom this collection might have taken far longer to complete.

The story "Interruptions" continues a thread from the novel *Missing Persons* (Toronto, ON: The Mercury Press, 2009), and is dedicated to Amanda Earl, who asked to know more. "Swimming lessons" is for Christine McNair. "The Matrix Resolutions" is for Stephen Brockwell. "The names of things," is for our late Alta Vista across-the-street neighbour, Ross Pryde (1965–2016).

Note: Gilles de Montmorency-Laval, Baron de Rais (1404–1440), included in the story "Silence," was posthumously exonerated for his crimes in 1992. For further information, check out English writer Margot K. Juby's website *Gilles de Rais Was Innocent*: http://gillesderaiswasinnocent.blogspot.co.uk/.

This book acknowledges the support of the Ontario Arts Council through the Writers' Reserve program (love best to Tightrope Books, Mansfield Press, Exile Editions, Insomniac Press, Invisible Publishing and *Taddle Creek*), and through a Writers' Works in Progress grant in 2015. This book also acknowledges the support of the City of Ottawa through their Creation and Production Fund for Professional Artists. Thanks to all for their continued assistance, and support of Canadian writing and culture.

And: while all characters included here are fictions, my friend Ian Jempson does appear briefly as himself in "Fourteen things you don't know about Arturus Booth." I thank him, despite the fact that I haven't actually informed him of this.

Deep thanks to Michelle Lobkowicz, Cathie Crooks and everyone else at University of Alberta Press. They do very good work, and it is a delight to not only rejoin their roster, but to be connected to any press that keeps Robert Kroetsch in print. Thanks, especially, to Kasia Van Schaik and Michael Trussler, who were my (originally, anonymous) readers via University of Alberta Press, providing both feedback and positive commentary, which allowed the manuscript to move toward publication. Grateful thanks to copyeditor Mary Lou Roy, as well, for the generous gift of her clarity.

Soundtrack: *Heroes* (1977), David Bowie; *Dive* (2011), Tycho; *Thursday Afternoon* (1985), Brian Eno.

December 2011–October 2018

Toronto–Ottawa–Sainte-Adèle–Ottawa